The Bet and Other Stories

ANTON CHEKHOV

Published by

Hawk Press
4836/24, Ansari Road, Daryaganj
New Delhi – 110 002
Phones: +91-11-23278618, +91-11-43667199
E-mail: thehawkpress@gmail.com
www.thehawkpress.com

ISBN: 978-93-88841-56-6

CONTENTS

THE BET

I

It was a dark autumn night. The old banker was pacing from corner to corner of his study, recalling to his mind the party he gave in the autumn fifteen years ago. There were many clever people at the party and much interesting conversation. They talked among other things of capital punishment. The guests, among them not a few scholars and journalists, for the most part disapproved of capital punishment. They found it obsolete as a means of punishment, unfitted to a Christian State and immoral. Some of them thought that capital punishment should be replaced universally by life-imprisonment.

"I don't agree with you," said the host. "I myself have experienced neither capital punishment nor life-imprisonment, but if one may judge a priori, then in my opinion capital punishment is more moral and more humane than imprisonment. Execution kills instantly, life-imprisonment kills by degrees. Who is the more humane executioner, one who kills you in a few seconds or one who draws the life out of you incessantly, for years?"

"They're both equally immoral," remarked one of the guests, "because their purpose is the same, to take away life. The State is not God. It has no right to take away that which it cannot give back, if it should so desire."

Among the company was a lawyer, a young man of about twenty-five. On being asked his opinion, he said:

"Capital punishment and life-imprisonment are equally immoral; but if I were offered the choice between them, I would certainly choose the second. It's better to live somehow than not to live at all."

There ensued a lively discussion. The banker who was then younger and more nervous suddenly lost his temper, banged his fist on the table, and turning to the young lawyer, cried out:

"It's a lie. I bet you two millions you wouldn't stick in a cell even for five years."

"If that's serious," replied the lawyer, "then I bet I'll stay not five but fifteen."

"Fifteen! Done!" cried the banker. "Gentlemen, I stake two millions."

"Agreed. You stake two millions, I my freedom," said the lawyer.

So this wild, ridiculous bet came to pass. The banker, who at that time had too many millions to count, spoiled and capricious, was beside himself with rapture. During supper he said to the lawyer jokingly:

"Come to your senses, young man, before it's too late. Two millions are nothing to me, but you stand to lose three or four of the best years of your life. I say three or four, because you'll never stick it out any longer. Don't forget either, you unhappy man, that voluntary is much heavier than enforced imprisonment. The idea that you have the right to free yourself at any moment will poison the whole of your life in the cell. I pity you."

And now the banker pacing from corner to corner, recalled all this and asked himself:

"Why did I make this bet? What's the good? The lawyer loses fifteen years of his life and I throw away two millions. Will it convince people that capital punishment is worse or better than imprisonment for life. No, No! all stuff and rubbish. On my part, it was the caprice of a well-fed man; on the lawyer's, pure greed of gold."

He recollected further what happened after the evening party. It was decided that the lawyer must undergo his imprisonment under the strictest observation, in a garden-wing of the banker's house. It was agreed that during the period he would be deprived of the right to cross the threshold, to see living people, to hear human voices, and to receive letters and newspapers. He was permitted to have a musical instrument, to read books, to write letters, to drink wine and smoke tobacco. By the agreement he could communicate, but only in silence, with the outside world through a little window specially constructed for this purpose. Everything necessary, books, music, wine, he could receive in any quantity by sending a note through the window. The agreement provided for all the minutest details, which made the confinement strictly solitary, and it obliged the lawyer to remain exactly fifteen years from twelve o'clock of November 14th 1870 to twelve o'clock of November 14th 1885. The least attempt on his part to violate the conditions, to escape if only for two minutes before the time freed the banker from the obligation to pay him the two millions.

During the first year of imprisonment, the lawyer, as far as it was possible to judge from his short notes, suffered terribly from loneliness and boredom. From his wing day and night came the sound of the piano. He rejected wine and tobacco. "Wine," he wrote, "excites desires, and desires are the chief foes of a prisoner; besides, nothing is more boring than to drink good wine alone," and tobacco spoils the air in his room. During the first year the lawyer was sent books of a light character; novels with a complicated love interest, stories of crime and fantasy, comedies, and so on.

In the second year the piano was heard no longer and the lawyer asked only for classics. In the fifth year, music was heard again, and the prisoner asked for wine. Those who watched him said that during the whole of that year he was only eating, drinking, and lying on his bed. He yawned often and talked angrily to himself. Books he did not read. Sometimes at nights he would sit down to write. He would write for a long time and tear it all up in the morning. More than once he was heard to weep.

In the second half of the sixth year, the prisoner began zealously to study languages, philosophy, and history. He fell on these subjects so hungrily that the banker hardly had time to get books enough for him. In the space of four years about six hundred volumes were bought at his request. It was while that passion lasted that the banker received the following letter from the prisoner: "My dear gaoler, I am writing these lines in six languages. Show them to experts. Let them read them. If they do not find one single mistake, I beg you to give orders to have a gun fired off in the garden. By the noise I shall know that my efforts have not been in vain. The geniuses of all ages and countries speak in different languages; but in them all burns the same flame. Oh, if you knew my heavenly happiness now that I can understand them!" The prisoner's desire was fulfilled. Two shots were fired in the garden by the banker's order.

Later on, after the tenth year, the lawyer sat immovable before his table and read only the New Testament. The banker found it strange that a man who in four years had mastered six hundred erudite volumes, should have spent nearly a year in reading one book, easy to understand

and by no means thick. The New Testament was then replaced by the history of religions and theology.

During the last two years of his confinement the prisoner read an extraordinary amount, quite haphazard. Now he would apply himself to the natural sciences, then would read Byron or Shakespeare. Notes used to come from him in which he asked to be sent at the same time a book on chemistry, a text-book of medicine, a novel, and some treatise on philosophy or theology. He read as though he were swimming in the sea among the broken pieces of wreckage, and in his desire to save his life was eagerly grasping one piece after another.

II

The banker recalled all this, and thought:

"To-morrow at twelve o'clock he receives his freedom. Under the agreement, I shall have to pay him two millions. If I pay, it's all over with me. I am ruined for ever...."

Fifteen years before he had too many millions to count, but now he was afraid to ask himself which he had more of, money or debts. Gambling on the Stock-Exchange, risky speculation, and the recklessness of which he could not rid himself even in old age, had gradually brought his business to decay; and the fearless, self-confident, proud man of business had become an ordinary banker, trembling at every rise and fall in the market.

"That cursed bet," murmured the old man clutching his head in despair.... "Why didn't the man die? He's only forty years old. He will take away my last farthing, marry, enjoy life, gamble on the Exchange, and I will look on like an envious beggar and hear the same words from him every day: 'I'm obliged to you for the happiness of my life. Let me help you.' No, it's too much! The only escape from bankruptcy and disgrace—is that the man should die."

The clock had just struck three. The banker was listening. In Ike house everyone was asleep, and one could hear only the frozen trees whining outside the windows. Trying to make no sound, he took out of his safe the key of the door which had not been opened for fifteen years, put on his overcoat, and went out of the house. The garden was dark and cold. It was raining. A keen damp wind hovered howling over all the garden and gave the trees no rest. Though he strained his eyes, the banker could see neither the ground, nor the white statues, nor the garden-wing, nor the trees. Approaching the place where the garden wing stood, he called the watchman twice. There was no answer. Evidently the watchman had taken shelter from the bad weather and was now asleep somewhere in the kitchen or the greenhouse.

"If I have the courage to fulfil my intention," thought the old man, "the suspicion will fall on the watchman first of all."

In the darkness he groped for the stairs and the door and entered the hall of the gardenwing, then poked his way into a narrow passage and struck a match. Not a soul was there. Someone's bed, with no bedclothes on it, stood there, and an iron stove was dark in the corner. The seals on the door that led into the prisoner's room were unbroken.

When the match went out, the old man, trembling from agitation, peeped into the little window.

In the prisoner's room a candle was burning dim. The prisoner himself sat by the table. Only his back, the hair on his head and his hands were visible. On the table, the two chairs, the carpet by the table open books were strewn.

Five minutes passed and the prisoner never once stirred. Fifteen years confinement had taught him to sit motionless. The banker tapped on the window with his finger, but the prisoner gave no movement in reply. Then the banker cautiously tore the seals from the door and put the key into the lock. The rusty lock gave a hoarse groan and the door creaked. The banker expected instantly to hear a cry of surprise and the sound of steps. Three minutes passed and it was as quiet behind the door as it had been before. He made up his mind to enter. Before the table sat a man, unlike an ordinary human being. It was a skeleton, with tight-drawn skin, with a woman's long curly hair, and a shaggy beard. The colour of his face was yellow, of an earthy shade; the cheeks were sunken, the back long and narrow, and the hand upon which he leaned his hairy head was so lean and skinny that it was painful to look upon. His hair was already silvering with grey, and no one who glanced at the senile emaciation of the face would have believed that he was only forty years old. On the table, before his bended head, lay a sheet of paper on which something was written in a tiny hand.

"Poor devil," thought the banker, "he's asleep and probably seeing millions in his dreams. I have only to take and throw this half-dead thing on the bed, smother him a moment with the pillow, and the most careful examination will find no trace of unnatural death. But, first, let us read what he has written here."

The banker took the sheet from the table and read:

"To-morrow at twelve o'clock midnight, I shall obtain my freedom and the right to mix with people. But before I leave this room and see the sun I think it necessary to say a few words to you. On my own clear conscience and before God who sees me I declare to you that I despise freedom, life, health, and all that your books call the blessings of the world.

"For fifteen years I have diligently studied earthly life. True, I saw neither the earth nor the people, but in your books I drank fragrant wine, sang songs, hunted deer and wild boar in the forests, loved women.... And beautiful women, like clouds ethereal, created by the magic of your poets' genius, visited me by night and whispered me wonderful tales, which made my head drunken. In your books I climbed the summits of Elbruz and Mont Blanc and saw from thence how the sun rose in the morning, and in the evening overflowed the sky, the ocean and the mountain ridges with a purple gold. I saw from thence how above me lightnings glimmered cleaving the clouds; I saw green forests, fields, rivers, lakes, cities; I heard syrens singing, and the playing of the pipes of Pan; I touched the wings of beautiful devils who came flying to me to speak of God.... In your books I cast myself into bottomless abysses, worked miracles, burned cities to the ground, preached new religions, conquered whole countries....

"Your books gave me wisdom. All that unwearying human thought created in the centuries is compressed to a little lump in my skull. I know that I am more clever than you all.

"And I despise your books, despise all wordly blessings and wisdom. Everything is void, frail, visionary and delusive like a mirage. Though you be proud and wise and beautiful, yet will death wipe you from the face of the earth like the mice underground; and your posterity, your history, and the immortality of your men of genius will be as frozen slag, burnt down together with the terrestrial globe.

"You are mad, and gone the wrong way. You take lie for truth and ugliness for beauty. You would marvel if by certain conditions there should suddenly grow on apple and orange trees, instead of fruit, frogs and lizards, and if roses should begin to breathe the odour of a sweating horse. So do I marvel at you, who have bartered heaven for earth. I do not want to understand you.

"That I may show you in deed my contempt for that by which you live, I waive the two millions of which I once dreamed as of paradise, and which I now despise. That I may deprive myself of my right to them, I shall come out from here five minutes before the stipulated term, and thus shall violate the agreement."

When he had read, the banker put the sheet on the table, kissed the head of the strange man, and began to weep. He went out of the wing. Never at any other time, not even after his terrible losses on the Exchange, had he felt such contempt for himself as now. Coming home, he lay down on his bed, but agitation and tears kept him long from sleep....

The next morning the poor watchman came running to him and told him that they had seen the man who lived in the wing climbing through the window into the garden. He had gone to the gate and disappeared. Together with his servants the banker went instantly to the wing and established the escape of his prisoner. To avoid unnecessary rumours he took the paper with the renunciation from the table and, on his return, locked it in his safe.

A TEDIOUS STORY

(FROM AN OLD MAN'S JOURNAL)

I

There lives in Russia an emeritus professor, Nicolai Stiepanovich... privy councillor and knight. He has so many Russian and foreign Orders that when he puts them on the students call him "the holy picture." His acquaintance is most distinguished. Not a single famous scholar lived or died during the last twenty-five or thirty years but he was intimately acquainted with him. Now he has no one to be friendly with, but speaking of the past the long list of his eminent friends would end with such names as Pirogov, Kavelin, and the poet Nekrasov, who bestowed upon him their warmest and most sincere friendship. He is a member of all the Russian and of three foreign universities, et cetera, et cetera. All this, and a great deal besides, forms what is known as my name.

This name of mine is very popular. It is known to every literate person in Russia; abroad it is mentioned from professorial chairs with the epithets "eminent and esteemed." It is reckoned among those fortunate names which to mention in vain or to abuse in public or in the Press is considered a mark of bad breeding. Indeed, it should be so; because with my name is inseparably associated the idea of a famous, richly gifted, and indubitably useful person. I am a steady worker, with the endurance of a camel, which is important. I am also endowed with talent, which is still more important. In passing, I would add that I am a well-educated, modest, and honest fellow. I have never poked my nose into letters or politics, never sought popularity in disputes with the ignorant, and made no speeches either at dinners or at my colleagues' funerals. Altogether there is not a single spot on my learned name, and it has nothing to complain of. It is fortunate.

The bearer of this name, that is myself, is a man of sixty-two, with a bald head, false teeth and an incurable tic. My name is as brilliant and prepossessing, as I, myself am dull and ugly. My head and hands tremble from weakness; my neck, like that of one of Turgeniev's heroines, resembles the handle of a counter-bass; my chest is hollow and my back narrow. When I speak or read my mouth twists, and when I smile my whole face is covered with senile, deathly wrinkles. There is nothing imposing in my pitiable face, save that when I suffer from the tic, I have a singular expression which compels anyone who looks at me to think: "This man will die soon, for sure."

I can still read pretty well; I can still hold the attention of my audience for two hours. My passionate manner, the literary form of my exposition and my humour make the defects of my voice almost unnoticeable, though it is dry, harsh, and hard like a hypocrite's. But I write badly. The part of my brain which governs the ability to write refused office. My memory has weakened, and my thoughts are too inconsequent; and when I expound them on paper, I always have a feeling that I have lost the sense of their organic connection. The construction is monotonous, and the sentence feeble and timid. I often do not write what I want to, and when I write the end I cannot remember the beginning. I often forget common words, and in writing a letter I always have to waste much energy in order to avoid superfluous sentences and unnecessary incidental statements; both bear clear witness of the decay of my intellectual activity. And it is remarkable that, the simpler the letter, the more tormenting is my effort. When writing a scientific article I fed much freer and much more intelligent than in writing a letter of welcome or a report. One thing more: it is easier for me to write German or English than Russian.

As regards my present life, I must first of all note insomnia, from which I have begun to suffer lately. If I were asked: "What is now the chief and fundamental fact of your existence?" I would answer: "Insomnia." From habit, I still undress at midnight precisely and get into bed. I soon fall asleep but wake just after one with the feeling that I have not slept at all. I must get out of bed and light the lamp. For an hour or two I walk about the room from corner to corner and inspect the long familiar pictures. When I am weary of walking I sit down to the table. I sit motionless thinking of nothing, feeling no desires; if a book lies before me I draw it mechanically towards me and read without interest. Thus lately in one night I read mechanically a whole novel with a strange title, "Of What the Swallow Sang." Or in order to occupy my attention I make myself count to a thousand, or I imagine the face of some one of my friends, and begin to remember in what year and under what circumstances he joined the faculty. I love to listen to sounds. Now, two rooms away from me my daughter Liza will say something quickly, in her sleep; then my wife will walk through the drawing-room with a candle and infallibly drop the box of matches. Then the shrinking wood of the cupboard squeaks or the burner of the lamp tinkles suddenly, and all these sounds somehow agitate me.

Not to sleep of nights confesses one abnormal; and therefore I wait impatiently for the morning and the day, when I have the right not to sleep. Many oppressive hours pass before the cock crows. He is my harbinger of good. As soon as he has crowed I know that in an hour's time the porter downstairs will awake and for some reason or other go up the stairs, coughing angrily; and later beyond the windows the air begins to pale gradually and voices echo in the street.

The day begins with the coming of my wife. She comes in to me in a petticoat, with her hair undone, but already washed and smelling of eau de Cologne, and looking as though she came in by accident, saying the same thing every time: "Pardon, I came in for a moment. You haven't slept again?" Then she puts the lamp out, sits by the table and begins to talk. I am not a prophet but I know beforehand what the subject of conversation will be, every morning the same. Usually, after breathless inquiries after my health, she suddenly remembers our son, the officer, who is serving in Warsaw. On the twentieth of each month we send him fifty roubles. This is our chief subject of conversation.

"Of course it is hard on us," my wife sighs. "But until he is finally settled we are obliged to help him. The boy is among strangers; the pay is small. But if you like, next month we'll send him forty roubles instead of fifty. What do you think?"

Daily experience might have convinced my wife that expenses do not grow less by talking of them. But my wife does not acknowledge experience and speaks about our officer punctually every day, about bread, thank Heaven, being cheaper and sugar a half-penny dearer—and all this in a tone as though it were news to me.

I listen and agree mechanically. Probably because I have not slept during the night strange idle thoughts take hold of me. I look at my wife and wonder like a child. In perplexity I ask myself: This old, stout, clumsy woman, with sordid cares and anxiety about bread and butter written in the dull expression of her face, her eyes tired with eternal thoughts of debts and poverty, who can talk only of expenses and smile only when things are cheap—was this once the slim Varya whom I loved passionately for her fine clear mind, her pure soul, her beauty, and as Othello loved Desdemona, for her "compassion" of my science? Is she really the same, my wife Varya, who bore me a son?

I gaze intently into the fat, clumsy old woman's face. I seek in her my Varya; but from the past nothing remains but her fear for my health and her way of calling my salary "our" salary and my hat "our" hat. It pains me to look at her, and to console her, if only a little, I let her talk as she pleases, and I am silent even when she judges people unjustly, or scolds me because I do not practise and do not publish text-books.

Our conversation always ends in the same way. My wife suddenly remembers that I have not yet had tea, and gives a start:

"Why am I sitting down?" she says, getting up. "The samovar has been on the table a long while, and I sit chatting. How forgetful I am? Good gracious!"

She hurries away, but stops at the door to say:

"We owe Yegor five months' wages. Do you realise it? It's a bad thing to let the servants' wages run on. I've said so often. It's much easier to pay ten roubles every month than fifty for five!"

Outside the door she stops again:

"I pity our poor Liza more than anybody. The girl studies at the Conservatoire. She's always in good society, and the Lord only knows how she's dressed. That fur-coat of hers! It's a sin to show yourself in the street in it. If she had a different father, it would do, but everyone knows he is a famous professor, a privy councillor."

So, having reproached me for my name and title, she goes away at last. Thus begins my day. It does not improve.

When I have drunk my tea, Liza comes in, in a fur-coat and hat, with her music, ready to go to the Conservatoire. She is twenty-two. She looks younger. She is pretty, rather like my wife when she was young. She kisses me tenderly on my forehead and my hand.

"Good morning, Papa. Quite well?"

As a child she adored ice-cream, and I often had to take her to a confectioner's. Ice-cream was her standard of beauty. If she wanted to praise me, she used to say: "Papa, you are ice-creamy." One finger she called the pistachio, the other the cream, the third the raspberry finger and so on. And when she came to say good morning, I used to lift her on to my knees and kiss her fingers, and say:

"The cream one, the pistachio one, the lemon one."

And now from force of habit I kiss Liza's fingers and murmur:

"Pistachio one, cream one, lemon one." But it does not sound the same. I am cold like the ice-cream and I feel ashamed. When my daughter comes in and touches my forehead with her lips I shudder as though a bee had stung my forehead, I smile constrainedly and turn away my face. Since my insomnia began a question has been driving like a nail into my brain. My daughter continually sees how terribly I, an old man, blush because I owe the servant his wages; she sees how often the worry of small debts forces me to leave my work and to pace the room from corner to corner for hours, thinking; but why hasn't she, even once, come to me without telling her mother and whispered: "Father, here's my watch, bracelets, earrings, dresses.... Pawn them all.... You need money"? Why, seeing how I and her mother try to hide our poverty, out of false pride—why does she not deny herself the luxury of music lessons? I would not accept the watch, the bracelets, or her sacrifices—God forbid!—I do not want that.

Which reminds me of my son, the Warsaw officer. He is a clever, honest, and sober fellow. But that doesn't mean very much. If I had an old father, and I knew that there were moments when he was ashamed of his poverty, I think I would give up my commission to someone else and hire myself out as a navvy. These thoughts of the children poison me. What good are they? Only a mean and irritable person Can take refuge in thinking evil of ordinary people because they are not heroes. But enough of that.

At a quarter to ten I have to go and lecture to my dear boys. I dress myself and walk the road I have known these thirty years. For me it has a history of its own. Here is a big grey building with a chemist's shop beneath. A tiny house once stood there, and it was a beer-shop. In this beer-shop I thought out my thesis, and wrote my first love-letter to Varya. I wrote it in pencil on a scrap of paper that began "Historia Morbi." Here is a grocer's shop. It used to belong to a little Jew who sold me cigarettes on credit, and later on to a fat woman who loved students "because every one of them had a mother." Now a red-headed merchant sits there, a very nonchalant man, who drinks tea from a copper tea-pot. And here are the gloomy gates of the University that have not been repaired for years; a weary porter in a sheepskin coat, a broom, heaps of snow ... Such gates cannot produce a good impression on a boy who comes fresh from the provinces and imagines that the temple of science is really a temple. Certainly, in the history of Russian pessimism, the age of university buildings, the dreariness of the corridors, the smoke-stains on the walls, the meagre light, the dismal appearance of the stairs, the clothes-pegs and the benches, hold one of the foremost places in the series of predisposing causes. Here is our garden. It does not seem to have grown any better or any worse since I was a student. I do not like it. It would be much more sensible if tall pine-trees and fine oaks grew there instead of consumptive lime-trees, yellow acacias and thin clipped lilac. The student's mood is created mainly by every one of the surroundings in which he studies; therefore he must see everywhere before him only what is great and strong and exquisite. Heaven preserve him from starveling trees, broken windows, and drab walls and doors covered with tom oilcloth.

As I approach my main staircase the door is open wide. I am met by my old friend, of the same age and name as I, Nicolas the porter. He grunts as he lets me in:

"It's frosty, Your Excellency."

Or if my coat is wet:

"It's raining a bit, Your Excellency."

Then he runs in front of me and opens all the doors on my way. In the study he carefully takes off my coat and at the same time manages to tell me some university news. Because of the close acquaintance that exists between all the University porters and keepers, he knows all that happens in the four faculties, in the registry, in the chancellor's cabinet, and the library. He knows everything. When, for instance, the resignation of the rector or dean is under discussion, I hear him talking to the junior porters, naming candidates and explaining offhand that so and so will not be approved by the Minister, so and so will himself refuse the honour; then he plunges into fantastic details of some mysterious papers received in the registry, of a secret conversation which appears to have taken place between the Minister and the curator, and so on. These details apart, he is almost always right. The impressions he forms of each candidate are original, but also true. If you want to know who read his thesis, joined the staff, resigned or died in a particular year, then you must seek the assistance of this veteran's colossal memory. He will not only name you the year, month, and day, but give you the accompanying details of this or any other event. Such memory is the privilege of love.

He is the guardian of the university traditions. From the porters before him he inherited many legends of the life of the university. He added to this wealth much of his own and if you like he will tell you many stories, long or short. He can tell you of extraordinary savants who knew everything, of remarkable scholars who did not sleep for weeks on end, of numberless martyrs to science; good triumphs over evil with him. The weak always conquer the strong, the wise man the fool, the modest the proud, the young the old. There is no need to take all these legends and stories for sterling; but filter them, and you will find what you want in your filter, a noble tradition and the names of true heroes acknowledged by all.

In our society all the information about the learned world consists entirely of anecdotes of the extraordinary absent-mindedness of old professors, and of a handful of jokes, which are ascribed to Guber or to myself or to Baboukhin. But this is too little for an educated society. If it loved science, savants and students as Nicolas loves them, it would long ago have had a literature of whole epics, stories, and biographies. But unfortunately this is yet to be.

The news told, Nicolas looks stem and we begin to talk business. If an outsider were then to hear how freely Nicolas uses the jargon, he would be inclined to think that he was a scholar, posing as a soldier. By the way, the rumours of the university-porter's erudition are very exaggerated. It is true that Nicolas knows more than a hundred Latin tags, can put a skeleton together and on occasion make a preparation, can make the students laugh with a long learned quotation, but the simple theory of the circulation of the blood is as dark to him now as it was twenty years ago.

At the table in my room, bent low over a book or a preparation, sits my dissector, Peter Ignatievich. He is a hardworking, modest man of thirty-five without any gifts, already bald and with a big belly. He works from morning to night, reads tremendously and remembers everything he has read. In this respect he is not merely an excellent man, but a man of gold; but in all others he is a cart-horse, or if you like a learned blockhead. The characteristic traits of a cart-horse which distinguish him from a creature of talent are these. His outlook is narrow, absolutely bounded by his specialism. Apart from his own subject he is as naive as a child. I remember once entering the room and saying:

"Think what bad luck! They say, Skobielev is dead."

Nicolas crossed himself; but Peter Ignatievich turned to me:

"Which Skobielev do you mean?"

Another time,—some time earlier—I announced that Professor Pierov was dead. That darling Peter Ignatievich asked:

"What was his subject?"

I imagine that if Patti sang into his ear, or Russia were attacked by hordes of Chinamen, or there was an earthquake, he would not lift a finger, but would go on in the quietest way with his eye screwed over his microscope. In a word: "What's Hecuba to him?" I would give anything to see how this dry old stick goes to bed with his wife.

Another trait: a fanatical belief in the infallibility of science, above all in everything that the Germans write. He is sure of himself and his preparations, knows the purpose of life, is absolutely ignorant of the doubts and disillusionments that turn talents grey,—a slavish worship of the authorities, and not a shadow of need to think for himself. It is hard to persuade him and quite impossible to discuss with him. Just try a discussion with a man who is profoundly convinced that the best science is medicine, the best men doctors, the best traditions—the medical! From the ugly past of medicine only one tradition has survived,—the white necktie that doctors wear still. For a learned, and more generally for an educated person there can exist only a general university tradition, without any division into traditions of medicine, of law, and so on. But it's quite impossible for Peter Ignatievich to agree with that; and he is ready to argue it with you till doomsday.

His future is quite plain to me. During the whole of his life he will make several hundred preparations of extraordinary purity, will write any number of dry, quite competent, essays, will make about ten scrupulously accurate translations; but he won't invent gunpowder. For gunpowder, imagination is wanted, inventiveness, and a gift for divination, and Peter Ignatievich has nothing of the kind. In short, he is not a master of science but a labourer.

Peter Ignatievich, Nicolas, and I whisper together. We are rather strange to ourselves. One feels something quite particular, when the audience booms like the sea behind the door. In thirty years I have not grown used to this feeling, and I have it every morning. I button up my frock-coat nervously, ask Nicolas unnecessary questions, get angry.... It is as though I were afraid; but it is not fear, but something else which I cannot name nor describe.

Unnecessarily, I look at my watch and say:

"Well, it's time to go."

And we march in, in this order: Nicolas with the preparations or the atlases in front, myself next, and after me, the cart-horse, modestly hanging his head; or, if necessary, a corpse on a stretcher in front and behind the corpse Nicolas and so on. The students rise when I appear, then sit down and the noise of the sea is suddenly still. Calm begins.

I know what I will lecture about, but I know nothing of how I will lecture, where I will begin and where I will end. There is not a single sentence ready in my brain. But as soon as I glance at the audience, sitting around me in an amphitheatre, and utter the stereotyped "In our last lecture we ended with...." and the sentences fly out of my soul in a long line—then it is full steam ahead. I speak with irresistible speed, and with passion, and it seems as though no earthly power could check the current of my speech. In order to lecture well, that is without being wearisome and to the listener's profit, besides talent you must have the knack of it and experience; you must have a clear idea both of your own powers, of the people to whom you are lecturing, and of the subject of your remarks. Moreover, you must be quick in the uptake, keep a sharp eye open, and never for a moment lose your field of vision.

When he presents the composer's thought, a good conductor does twenty things at once. He reads the score, waves his baton, watches the singer makes a gesture now towards the drum, now to the double-bass, and so on. It is the same with me when lecturing. I have some hundred and fifty faces before me, quite unlike each other, and three hundred eyes staring me straight in the face. My purpose is to conquer this many-headed hydra. If I have a clear idea how far they are attending and how much they are comprehending every minute while I am lecturing, then the hydra is in my power. My other opponent is within me. This is the endless variety of forms, phenomena and laws, and the vast number of ideas, whether my own or others', which depend upon them. Every moment I must be skilful enough to choose what is most important and necessary from this enormous material, and just as swiftly as my speech flows to clothe my thought in a form which will penetrate the hydra's understanding and excite its attention. Besides I must watch carefully to see that my thoughts shall not be presented as they have been accumulated, but in a certain order, necessary for the correct composition of the picture which I wish to paint. Further, I endeavour to make my speech literary, my definitions brief and exact, my sentences as simple and elegant as possible. Every moment I must hold myself in and remember that I have only an hour and forty minutes to spend. In other words, it is a heavy labour. At one and the same time you have to be a savant, a schoolmaster, and an orator, and it is a failure if the orator triumphs over the schoolmaster in you or the schoolmaster over the orator.

After lecturing for a quarter, for half an hour, I notice suddenly that the students have begun to stare at the ceiling or Peter Ignatievich. One will feel for his handkerchief, another settle himself comfortably, another smile at his own thoughts. This means their attention is tried. I must take steps. I seize the first opening and make a pun. All the hundred and fifty faces have a broad smile, their eyes flash merrily, and for a while you can hear the boom of the sea. I laugh too. Their attention is refreshed and I can go on.

No sport, no recreation, no game ever gave me such delight as reading a lecture. Only in a lecture could I surrender myself wholly to passion and understand that inspiration is not a poet's fiction, but exists indeed. And I do not believe that Hercules, even after the most delightful of his exploits, felt such a pleasant weariness as I experienced every time after a lecture.

This was in the past. Now at lectures I experience only torture. Not half an hour passes before I begin to feel an invincible weakness in my legs and shoulders. I sit down in my chair, but I am not used to lecture sitting. In a moment I am up again, and lecture standing. Then I sit down again. Inside my mouth is dry, my voice is hoarse, my head feels dizzy. To hide my state from my audience I drink some water now and then, cough, wipe my nose continually, as though I was troubled by a cold, make inopportune puns, and finally announce the interval earlier than I should. But chiefly I feel ashamed.

Conscience and reason tell me that the best thing I could do now is to read my farewell lecture to the boys, give them my last word, bless them and give up my place to someone younger and stronger than I. But, heaven be my judge, I have not the courage to act up to my conscience.

Unfortunately, I am neither philosopher nor theologian. I know quite well I have no more than six months to live; and it would seem that now I ought to be mainly occupied with questions of the darkness beyond the grave, and the visions which will visit my sleep in the earth. But somehow my soul is not curious of these questions, though my mind grants every atom of their importance. Now before my death it is just as it was twenty or thirty years ago. Only science interests me.—When I take my last breath I shall still believe that Science is the most important, the most beautiful, the most necessary thing in the life of man; that she has always been and always will be the highest manifestation of love, and that by her alone will man triumph over nature and himself. This faith is, perhaps, at bottom naive and unfair, but I am not to blame if this and not another is my faith. To conquer this faith within me is for me impossible.

But this is beside the point. I only ask that you should incline to my weakness and understand that to tear a man who is more deeply concerned with the destiny of a brain tissue than the final goal of creation away from his rostrum and his students is like taking him and nailing him up in a coffin without waiting until he is dead.

Because of my insomnia and the intense struggle with my increasing weakness a strange thing happens inside me. In the middle of my lecture tears rise to my throat, my eyes begin to ache, and I have a passionate and hysterical desire to stretch out my hands and moan aloud. I want to cry out that fate has doomed me, a famous man, to death; that in some six months here in the auditorium another will be master. I want to cry out that I am poisoned; that new ideas that I did not know before have poisoned the last days of my life, and sting my brain incessantly like mosquitoes. At that moment my position seems so terrible to me that I want all my students to be terrified, to jump from their seats and rush panic-stricken to the door, shrieking in despair.

It is not easy to live through such moments.

II

After the lecture I sit at home and work. I read reviews, dissertations, or prepare for the next lecture, and sometimes I write something. I work with interruptions, since I have to receive visitors.

The bell rings. It is a friend who has come to talk over some business. He enters with hat and stick. He holds them both in front of him and says:

"Just a minute, a minute. Sit down, cher confrère. Only a word or two."

First we try to show each other that we are both extraordinarily polite and very glad to see each other. I make him sit down in the chair, and he makes me sit down; and then we touch each other's waists, and put our hands on each other's buttons, as though we were feeling each other and afraid to bum ourselves. We both laugh, though we say nothing funny. Sitting down, we bend our heads together and begin to whisper to each other. We must gild our conversation with such Chinese formalities as: "You remarked most justly" or "I have already had the occasion to say." We must giggle if either of us makes a pun, though it's a bad one. When we have finished with the business, my friend gets up with a rush, waves his hat towards my work, and begins to take his leave. We feel each other once more and laugh. I accompany him down to the hall. There I help my friend on with his coat, but he emphatically declines so great an honour. Then, when Yegor opens the door my friend assures me that I will catch cold, and I pretend to be ready to follow him into the street. And when I finally return to my study my face keeps smiling still, it must be from inertia.

A little later another ring. Someone enters the hall, spends a long time taking off his coat and coughs. Yegor brings me word that a student has come. I tell him to show him up. In a minute a pleasant-faced young man appears. For a year we have been on these forced terms together. He sends in abominable answers at examinations, and I mark him gamma. Every year I have about seven of these people to whom, to use the students' slang, "I give a plough" or "haul them through." Those of them who fail because of stupidity or illness, usually bear their cross in patience and do not bargain with me; only sanguine temperaments, "open natures," bargain with me and come to my house, people whose appetite is spoiled or who are prevented from going regularly to the opera by a delay in their examinations. With the first I am over-indulgent; the second kind I keep on the run for a year.

"Sit down," I say to my guest. "What was it you wished to say?"

"Forgive me for troubling you, Professor...." he begins, stammering and never looking me in the face. "I would not venture to trouble you unless.... I was up for my examination before you for the fifth time ... and I failed. I implore you to be kind, and give me a 'satis,' because...."

The defence which all idlers make of themselves is always the same. They have passed in every other subject with distinction, and failed only in mine, which is all the more strange because they had always studied my subject most diligently and know it thoroughly. They failed through some inconceivable misunderstanding.

"Forgive me, my friend," I say to my guest. "But I can't give you a 'satis'—impossible. Go and read your lectures again, and then come. Then we'll see."

Pause. I get a desire to torment the student a little, because he prefers beer and the opera to science; and I say with a sigh:

"In my opinion, the best thing for you now is to give up the Faculty of Medicine altogether. With your abilities, if you find it impossible to pass the examination, then it seems you have neither the desire nor the vocation to be a doctor."

My sanguine friend's face grows grave.

"Excuse me, Professor," he smiles, "but it would be strange, to say the least, on my part. Studying medicine for five years and suddenly—to throw it over."

"Yes, but it's better to waste five years than to spend your whole life afterwards in an occupation which you dislike."

Immediately I begin to feel sorry for him and hasten to say:

"Well, do as you please. Read a little and come again."

"When?" the idler asks, dully.

"Whenever you like. To-morrow, even."

And I read in his pleasant eyes. "I can come again; but you'll send me away again, you beast."

"Of course," I say, "you won't become more learned because you have to come up to me fifteen times for examination; but this will form your character. You must be thankful for that."

Silence. I rise and wait for my guest to leave. But he stands there, looking at the window, pulling at his little beard and thinking. It becomes tedious.

My sanguine friend has a pleasant, succulent voice, clever, amusing eyes, a good-natured face, rather puffed by assiduity to beer and much resting on the sofa. Evidently he could tell me many interesting things about the opera, about his love affairs, about the friends he adores; but, unfortunately, it is not the thing. And I would so eagerly listen!

"On my word of honour, Professor, if you give me a 'satis' I'll...."

As soon as it gets to "my word of honour," I wave my hands and sit down to the table. The student thinks for a while and says, dejectedly:

"In that case, good-bye.... Forgive me!"

"Good-bye, my friend.... Good-bye!"

He walks irresolutely into the hall, slowly puts on his coat, and, when he goes into the street, probably thinks again for a long while; having excogitated nothing better than "old devil" for me, he goes to a cheap restaurant to drink beer and dine, and then home to sleep. Peace be to your ashes, honest labourer!

A third ring. Enters a young doctor in a new black suit, gold-rimmed spectacles and the inevitable white necktie. He introduces himself. I ask him to take a seat and inquire his business. The young priest of science begins to tell me, not without agitation, that he passed his doctor's examination this year, and now has only to write his dissertation. He would like to work with me, under my guidance; and I would do him a great kindness if I would suggest a subject for his dissertation.

"I should be delighted to be of use to you, mon cher confrère," I say. "But first of all, let us come to an agreement as to what is a dissertation. Generally we understand by this, work produced as the result of an independent creative power. Isn't that so? But a work written on another's subject, under another's guidance, has a different name."

The aspirant is silent. I fire up and jump out of my seat. "Why do you all come to me? I can't understand," I cry out angrily. "Do I keep a shop? I don't sell theses across the counter. For the one thousandth time I ask you all to leave me alone. Forgive my rudeness, but I've got tired of it at last!"

The aspirant is silent. Only, a tinge of colour shows on his cheek. His face expresses his profound respect for my famous name and my erudition, but I see in his eyes that he despises my voice, my pitiable figure, my nervous gestures. When I am angry I seem to him a very queer fellow.

"I do not keep a shop," I storm. "It's an amazing business! Why don't you want to be independent? Why do you find freedom so objectionable?"

I say a great deal, but he is silent. At last by degrees I grow calm, and, of course, surrender. The aspirant will receive a valueless subject from me, will write under my observation a needless thesis, will pass his tedious disputation cum laude and will get a useless and learned degree.

The rings follow in endless succession, but here I confine myself to four. The fourth ring sounds, and I hear the familiar steps, the rustling dress, the dear voice.

Eighteen years ago my dear friend, the oculist, died and left behind him a seven year old daughter, Katy, and sixty thousand roubles. By his will he made me guardian. Katy lived in my family till she was ten. Afterwards she was sent to College and lived with me only in her holidays in the summer months. I had no time to attend to her education. I watched only by fits and starts; so that I can say very little about her childhood.

The chief thing I remember, the one I love to dwell upon in memory, is the extraordinary confidence which she had when she entered my house, when she had to have the doctor,—a confidence which was always shining in her darling face. She would sit in a corner somewhere with her face tied up, and would be sure to be absorbed in watching something. Whether she was watching me write and read books, or my wife bustling about, or the cook peeling the potatoes in the kitchen or the dog playing about—her eyes invariably expressed the same thing: "Everything that goes on in this world,—everything is beautiful and clever." She was inquisitive and adored to talk to me. She would sit at the table opposite me, watching my movements and asking questions. She is interested to know what I read, what I do at the University, if I'm not afraid of corpses, what I do with my money.

"Do the students fight at the University?" she would ask.

"They do, my dear."

"You make them go down on their knees?"

"I do."

And it seemed funny to her that the students fought and that I made them go down on their knees, and she laughed. She was a gentle, good, patient child.

Pretty often I happened to see how something was taken away from her, or she was unjustly punished, or her curiosity was not satisfied. At such moments sadness would be added to her permanent expression of confidence—nothing more. I didn't know how to take her part, but when I saw her sadness, I always had the desire to draw her close to me and comfort her in an old nurse's voice: "My darling little orphan!"

I remember too she loved to be well dressed and to sprinkle herself with scents. In this she was like me. I also love good clothes and fine scents.

I regret that I had neither the time nor the inclination to watch the beginnings and the growth of the passion which had completely taken hold of Katy when she was no more than fourteen or fifteen. I mean her passionate love for the theatre. When she used to come from the College for her holidays and live with us, nothing gave her such pleasure and enthusiasm to talk about as plays and actors. She used to tire us with her incessant conversation about the theatre. I alone hadn't the courage to deny her my attention. My wife and children did not listen to her. When she felt the desire to share her raptures she would come to my study and coax: "Nicolai Stiepanich, do let me speak to you about the theatre."

I used to show her the time and say:

"I'll give you half an hour. Fire away!"

Later on she used to bring in pictures of the actors and actresses she worshipped—whole dozens of them. Then several times she tried to take part in amateur theatricals, and finally when she left College she declared to me she was born to be an actress.

I never shared Katy's enthusiasms for the theatre. My opinion is that if a play is good then there's no need to trouble the actors for it to make the proper impression; you can be satisfied merely by reading it. If the play is bad, no acting will make it good.

When I was young I often went to the theatre, and nowadays my family takes a box twice a year and carries me off for an airing there. Of course this is not enough to give me the right to pass verdicts on the theatre; but I will say a few words about it. In my opinion the theatre hasn't improved in the last thirty or forty years. I can't find any more than I did then, a glass of dean water, either in the corridors or the foyer. Just as they did then, the attendants fine me sixpence for my coat, though there's nothing illegal in wearing a warm coat in winter. Just as it did then, the orchestra plays quite unnecessarily in the intervals, and adds a new, gratuitous impression to the one received from the play. Just as they did then, men go to the bar in the intervals and drink spirits. If there is no perceptible improvement in little things, it will be useless to look for it in the bigger things. When an actor, hide-bound in theatrical traditions and prejudices, tries to read simple straightforward monologue: "To be or not to be," not at all simply, but with an incomprehensible and inevitable hiss and convulsions over his whole body, or when he tries to convince me that Chazky, who is always talking to fools and is in love with a fool, is a very clever man and that "The Sorrows of Knowledge" is not a boring play,—then I get from the stage a breath of the same old routine that exasperated me forty years ago when I was regaled with classical lamentation and beating on the breast. Every time I come out of the theatre a more thorough conservative than I went in.

It's quite possible to convince the sentimental, self-confident crowd that the theatre in its present state is an education. But not a man who knows what true education is would swallow this. I don't know what it may be in fifty or a hundred years, but under present conditions the theatre can only be a recreation. But the recreation is too expensive for continual use, and robs the country of thousands of young, healthy, gifted men and women, who if they had not devoted themselves to the theatre would be excellent doctors, farmers, schoolmistresses, or officers. It robs the public of its evenings, the best time for intellectual work and friendly conversation. I pass over the waste of money and the moral injuries to the spectator when he sees murder, adultery, or slander wrongly treated on the stage.

But Katy's opinion was quite the opposite. She assured me that even in its present state the theatre is above lecture-rooms and books, above everything else in the world. The theatre is a power that unites in itself all the arts, and the actors are men with a mission. No separate art or science can act on the human soul so strongly and truly as the stage; and therefore it is reasonable that a medium actor should enjoy much greater popularity than the finest scholar or painter. No public activity can give such delight and satisfaction as the theatrical.

So one fine day Katy joined a theatrical company and went away, I believe, to Ufa, taking with her a lot of money, a bagful of rainbow hopes, and some very high-class views on the business.

Her first letters on the journey were wonderful. When I read them I was simply amazed that little sheets of paper could contain so much youth, such transparent purity, such divine innocence, and at the same time so many subtle, sensible judgments, that would do honour to a sound masculine intelligence. The Volga, nature, the towns she visited, her friends, her successes and failures—she did not write about them, she sang. Every line breathed the confidence which I used to see in her face; and with all this a mass of grammatical mistakes and hardly a single stop.

Scarce six months passed before I received a highly poetical enthusiastic letter, beginning, "I have fallen in love." She enclosed a photograph of a young man with a clean-shaven face, in a broad-brimmed hat, with a plaid thrown over his shoulders. The next letters were just as splendid, but stops already began to appear and the grammatical mistakes to vanish. They had a strong masculine scent. Katy began to write about what a good thing it would be to build a big theatre somewhere in the Volga, but on a cooperative basis, and to attract the rich business-men and shipowners to the undertaking. There would be plenty of money, huge receipts, and the actors would work in partnership.... Perhaps all this is really a good thing, but I can't help thinking such schemes could only come from a man's head.

Anyhow for eighteen months or a couple of years everything seemed to be all right. Katy was in love, had her heart in her business and was happy. But later on I began to notice dear symptoms of a decline in her letters. It began with Katy complaining about her friends. This is the first and most ominous sign. If a young scholar or litterateur begins his career by complaining bitterly about other scholars or littérateurs, it means that he is tired already and not fit for his business. Katy wrote to me that her friends would not come to rehearsals and never knew their parts; that they showed an utter contempt for the public in the absurd plays they staged and the manner they behaved. To swell the box-office receipts—the only topic of conversation—serious actresses degrade themselves by singing sentimentalities, and tragic actors sing music-hall songs, laughing at husbands who are deceived and unfaithful wives who are pregnant. In short, it was amazing that the profession, in the provinces, was not absolutely dead. The marvel was that it could exist at all with such thin, rotten blood in its veins.

In reply I sent Katy a long and, I confess, a very tedious letter. Among other things I wrote: "I used to talk fairly often to actors in the past, men of the noblest character, who honoured me with their friendship. From my conversations with them I understood that their activities were guided rather by the whim and fashion of society than by the free working of their own minds. The best of them in their lifetime had to play in tragedy, in musical comedy, in French farce, and in pantomime; yet all through they considered that they were treading the right path and being useful. You see that this means that you must look for the cause of the evil, not in the actors, but deeper down, in the art itself and the attitude of society towards it." This letter of mine only made Katy cross. "You and I are playing in different operas. I didn't write to you about men of the noblest character, but about a lot of sharks who haven't a spark of nobility in them. They are a horde of savages who came on the stage only because they wouldn't be allowed anywhere else. The only ground they have for calling themselves artists is their impudence. Not a single talent among them, but any number of incapables, drunkards, intriguers, and slanderers. I can't tell you how bitterly I feel it that the art I love so much is fallen into the hands of people I despise. It hurts me that the best men should be content to look at evil from a distance and not want to come nearer. Instead of taking an active part, they write ponderous platitudes and useless sermons...." and more in the same strain.

A little while after I received the following: "I have been inhumanly deceived. I can't go on living any more. Do as you think fit with my money. I loved you as a father and as my only friend. Forgive me."

So it appeared that he too belonged to the horde of savages. Later on, I gathered from various hints, that there was an attempt at suicide. Apparently, Katy tried to poison herself. I think she must have been seriously ill afterwards, for I got the following letter from Yalta, where most probably the doctors had sent her. Her last letter to me contained a request that I should send her at Yalta a thousand roubles, and it ended with the words: "Forgive me for writing such a sad letter. I buried my baby yesterday." After she had spent about a year in the Crimea she returned home.

She had been travelling for about four years, and during these four years I confess that I occupied a strange and unenviable position in regard to her. When she announced to me that she was going on to the stage and afterwards wrote to me about her love; when the desire to spend took hold of her, as it did periodically, and I had to send her every now and then one or two thousand roubles at her request; when she wrote that she intended to die, and afterwards that her baby was dead,—-I was at a loss every time. All my sympathy with her fate consisted in thinking hard and writing long tedious letters which might as well never have been written. But then I was in loco parentis and I loved her as a daughter.

Katy lives half a mile away from me now. She took a five-roomed house and furnished it comfortably, with the taste that was born in her. If anyone were to undertake to depict her surroundings, then the dominating mood of the picture would be indolence. Soft cushions, soft chairs for her indolent body; carpets for her indolent feet; faded, dim, dull colours for her indolent eyes; for her indolent soul, a heap of cheap fans and tiny pictures on the walls, pictures in which novelty of execution was more noticeable than content; plenty of little tables and stands, set out with perfectly useless and worthless things, shapeless scraps instead of curtains.... All this, combined with a horror of bright colours, of symmetry, and space, betokened a perversion of the natural taste as well as indolence of the soul. For whole days Katy lies on the sofa and reads books, mostly novels and stories. She goes outside her house but once in the day, to come and see me.

I work. Katy sits on the sofa at my side. She is silent, and wraps herself up in her shawl as though she were cold. Either because she is sympathetic to me, or I because I had got used to her continual visits while she was still a little girl, her presence does not prevent me from concentrating on my work. At long intervals I ask her some question or other, mechanically, and she answers very curtly; or, for a moment's rest, I turn towards her and watch how she is absorbed in looking through some medical review or newspaper. And then I see that the old expression of confidence in her face is there no more. Her expression now is cold, indifferent, distracted, like that of a passenger who has to wait a long while for his train. She dresses as she used—well and simply, but carelessly. Evidently her clothes and her hair suffer not a little from the sofas and hammocks on which she lies for days together. And she is not curious any more. She doesn't ask me questions any more, as if she had experienced everything in life and did not expect to hear anything new.

About four o'clock there is a sound of movement in the hall and the drawing-room. It's Liza come back from the Conservatoire, bringing her friends with her. You can hear them playing the piano, trying their voices and giggling. Yegor is laying the table in the dining-room and making a noise with the plates.

"Good-bye," says Katy. "I shan't go in to see your people. They must excuse me. I haven't time. Come and see me."

When I escort her into the hall, she looks me over sternly from head to foot, and says in vexation:

"You get thinner and thinner. Why don't you take a cure? I'll go to Sergius Fiodorovich and ask him to come. You must let him see you."

"It's not necessary, Katy."

"I can't understand why your family does nothing. They're a nice lot."

She puts on her jacket with her rush. Inevitably, two or three hair-pins fall out of her careless hair on to the floor. It's too much bother to tidy her hair now; besides she is in a hurry. She pushes the straggling strands of hair untidily under her hat and goes away.

As soon as I come into the dining-room, my wife asks:

"Was that Katy with you just now? Why didn't she come to see us. It really is extraordinary...."

"Mamma!" says Liza reproachfully, "If she doesn't want to come, that's her affair. There's no need for us to go on our knees."

"Very well; but it's insulting. To sit in the study for three hours, without thinking of us. But she can do as she likes."

Varya and Liza both hate Katy. This hatred is unintelligible to me; probably you have to be a woman to understand it. I'll bet my life on it that you'll hardly find a single one among the hundred and fifty young men I see almost every day in my audience, or the hundred old ones I happen to meet every week, who would be able to understand why women hate and abhor Katy's past, her being pregnant and unmarried and her illegitimate child. Yet at the same time I cannot bring to mind a single woman or girl of my acquaintance who would not cherish such feelings, either consciously or instinctively. And it's not because women are purer and more virtuous than men. If virtue and purity are not free from evil feeling, there's precious little difference between them and vice. I explain it simply by the backward state of women's development. The sorrowful sense of compassion and the torment of conscience, which the modern man experiences when he sees distress have much more to tell me about culture and moral development than have hatred and repulsion. The modern woman is as lachrymose and as coarse in heart as she was in the middle ages. And in my opinion those who advise her to be educated like a man have wisdom on their side.

But still my wife does not like Katy, because she was an actress, and for her ingratitude, her pride, her extravagances, and all the innumerable vices one woman can always discover in another.

Besides myself and my family we have two or three of my daughter's girl friends to dinner and Alexander Adolphovich Gnekker, Liza's admirer and suitor. He is a fair young man, not more than thirty years old, of middle height, very fat, broad shouldered, with reddish hair round his ears and a little stained moustache, which give his smooth chubby face the look of a doll's. He wears a very short jacket, a fancy waistcoat, large-striped trousers, very full on the hip and very narrow in the leg, and brown boots without heels. His eyes stick out like a lobster's, his tie is like a lobster's tail, and I can't help thinking even that the smell of lobster soup clings about the whole of this young man. He visits us every day; but no one in the family knows where he comes from, where he was educated, or how he lives. He cannot play or sing, but he has a certain connection with music as well as singing, for he is agent for somebody's pianos, and is often at the Academy. He knows all the celebrities, and he manages concerts. He gives his opinion on music with great authority and I have noticed that everybody hastens to agree with him.

Rich men always have parasites about them. So do the sciences and the arts. It seems that there is no science or art in existence, which is free from such "foreign bodies" as this Mr. Gnekker. I am not a musician and perhaps I am mistaken about Gnekker, besides I don't know him very well. But I can't help suspecting the authority and dignity with which he stands beside the piano and listens when anyone is singing or playing.

You may be a gentleman and a privy councillor a hundred times over; but if you have a daughter you can't be guaranteed against the pettinesses that are so often brought into your house and into your own humour, by courtings, engagements, and weddings. For instance, I cannot reconcile myself to my wife's solemn expression every time Gnekker comes to our house, nor to those bottles of Château Lafitte, port, and sherry which are put on the table only for him, to convince him beyond doubt of the generous luxury in which we live. Nor can I stomach the staccato laughter which Liza learned at the Academy, and her way of screwing up her eyes, when men are about the house. Above all, I can't understand why it is that such a creature should come to me every day and have dinner with me—a creature perfectly foreign to my habits, my science, and the whole tenour of my life, a creature absolutely unlike the men I love. My wife and the servants whisper mysteriously that that is "the bridegroom," but still I can't understand why he's there. It disturbs my mind just as much as if a Zulu were put next to me at table. Besides, it seems strange to me that my daughter whom I used to think of as a baby should be in love with that necktie, those eyes, those chubby cheeks.

Formerly, I either enjoyed my dinner or was indifferent about it. Now it does nothing but bore and exasperate me. Since I was made an Excellency and Dean of the Faculty, for some reason or other my family found it necessary to make a thorough change in our menu and the dinner arrangements. Instead of the simple food I was used to as a student and a doctor, I am now fed on potage-puree, with some sossoulki swimming about in it, and kidneys in Madeira. The title of General and my renown have robbed me for ever of schi and savoury pies, and roast goose with apple sauce, and bream with kasha. They robbed me as well of my maid servant Agasha, a funny, talkative old woman, instead of whom I am now waited on by Yegor, a stupid, conceited fellow who always has a white glove in his right hand. The intervals between the courses are short, but they seem terribly long. There is nothing to fill them. We don't have any more of the old good-humour, the familiar conversations, the jokes and the laughter; no more mutual endearments, or the gaiety that used to animate my children, my wife, and myself when we met at the dinner table. For a busy man like me dinner was a time to rest and meet my friends, and a feast for my wife and children, not a very long feast, to be sure, but a gay and happy one, for they knew that for half an hour I did not belong to science and my students, but solely to them and to no one else. No more chance of getting tipsy on a single glass of wine, no more Agasha, no more bream with kasha, no more the old uproar to welcome our little contretemps at dinner, when the cat fought the dog under the table, or Katy's head-band fell down her cheek into her soup.

Our dinner nowadays is as nasty to describe as to eat. On my wife's face there is pompousness, an assumed gravity, and the usual anxiety. She eyes our plates nervously: "I see you don't like the meat?... Honestly, don't you like it?" And I must answer, "Don't worry, my dear. The meat is very good." She: "You're always taking my part, Nicolai Stiepanich. You never tell the truth. Why has Alexander Adolphovich eaten so little?" and the same sort of conversation for the whole of dinner. Liza laughs staccato and screws up her eyes. I look at both of them, and at this moment at dinner here I can see quite clearly that their inner lives have slipped out of my observation long ago. I feel as though once upon a time I lived at home with a real family, but now I am dining as a guest with an unreal wife and looking at an unreal Liza. There has been an utter change in both of them, while I have lost sight of the long process that led up to the change. No wonder I don't understand anything. What was the reason of the change? I don't know. Perhaps the only trouble is that God did not give my wife and daughter the strength He gave me. From my childhood I have been accustomed to resist outside influences and have been hardened enough. Such earthly catastrophes as fame, being made General, the change from comfort to living above my means, acquaintance with high society, have scarcely touched me. I have survived safe and sound. But it all fell down like an avalanche on my weak, unhardened wife and Liza, and crushed them.

Gnekker and the girls talk of fugues and counter-fugues; singers and pianists, Bach and Brahms, and my wife, frightened of being suspected of musical ignorance, smiles sympathetically and murmurs: "Wonderful.... Is it possible?... Why?..." Gnekker eats steadily, jokes gravely, and listens condescendingly to the ladies' remarks. Now and then he has the desire to talk bad French, and then he finds it necessary for some unknown reason to address me magnificently, "Votre Excellence."

And I am morose. Apparently I embarrass them all and they embarrass me. I never had any intimate acquaintance with class antagonism before, but now something of the kind torments me indeed. I try to find only bad traits in Gnekker. It does not take long and then I am tormented because one of my friends has not taken his place as bridegroom. In another way too his presence has a bad effect upon me. Usually, when I am left alone with myself or when I am in the company of people I love, I never think of my merits; and if I begin to think about them they seem as trivial as though I had become a scholar only yesterday. But in the presence of a man like Gnekker my merits appear to me like an extremely high mountain, whose summit is lost in the clouds, while Gnekkers move about the foot, so small as hardly to be seen.

After dinner I go up to my study and light my little pipe, the only one during the whole day, the sole survivor of my old habit of smoking from morning to night. My wife comes into me while I am smoking and sits down to speak to me. Just as in the morning, I know beforehand what the conversation will be.

"We ought to talk seriously, Nicolai Stiepanovich," she begins. "I mean about Liza. Why won't you attend?"

"Attend to what?"

"You pretend you don't notice anything. It's not right: It's not right to be unconcerned. Gnekker has intentions about Liza. What do you say to that?"

"I can't say he's a bad man, because I don't know him; but I've told you a thousand times already that I don't like him."

"But that's impossible ... impossible...." She rises and walks about in agitation.

"It's impossible to have such an attitude to a serious matter," she says. "When our daughter's happiness is concerned, we must put everything personal aside. I know you don't like him.... Very well.... But if we refuse him now and upset everything, how can you guarantee that Liza won't have a grievance against us for the rest of her life? Heaven knows there aren't many young men nowadays. It's quite likely there won't be another chance. He loves Liza very much and she likes him, evidently. Of course he hasn't a settled position. But what is there to do? Please God, he'll get a position in time. He comes of a good family, and he's rich."

"How did you find that out?"

"He said so himself. His father has a big house in Kharkov and an estate outside. You must certainly go to Kharkov."

"Why?"

"You'll find out there. You have acquaintances among the professors there. I'd go myself. But I'm a woman. I can't."

"I will not go to Kharkov," I say morosely.

My wife gets frightened; a tormented expression comes over her face.

"For God's sake, Nicolai Stiepanich," she implores, sobbing, "For God's sake help me with this burden! It hurts me."

It is painful to look at her.

"Very well, Varya," I say kindly, "If you like—very well I'll go to Kharkov, and do everything you want."

She puts her handkerchief to her eyes and goes to cry in her room. I am left alone.

A little later they bring in the lamp. The familiar shadows that have wearied me for years fall from the chairs and the lamp-shade on to the walls and the floor. When I look at them it seems that it's night already, and the cursed insomnia has begun. I lie down on the bed; then I get up and walk about the room then lie down again. My nervous excitement generally reaches its highest after dinner, before the evening. For no reason I begin to cry and hide my head in the pillow. All the while I am afraid somebody may come in; I am afraid I shall die suddenly; I am ashamed of my tears; altogether, something intolerable is happening in my soul. I feel I cannot look at the lamp or the books or the shadows on the floor, or listen to the voices in the drawing-room any more. Some invisible, mysterious force pushes me rudely out of my house. I jump up, dress hurriedly, and go cautiously out into the street so that the household shall not notice me. Where shall I go?

The answer to this question has long been there in my brain: "To Katy."

III

As usual she is lying on the Turkish divan or the couch and reading something. Seeing me she lifts her head languidly, sits down, and gives me her hand.

"You are always lying down like that," I say after a reposeful silence. "It's unhealthy. You'd far better be doing something."

"Ah?"

"You'd far better be doing something, I say."

"What?... A woman can be either a simple worker or an actress."

"Well, then—if you can't become a worker, be an actress."

She is silent.

"You had better marry," I say, half-joking.

"There's no one to marry: and no use if I did."

"You can't go on living like this."

"Without a husband? As if that mattered. There are as many men as you like, if you only had the will."

"This isn't right, Katy."

"What isn't right?"

"What you said just now."

Katy sees that I am chagrined, and desires to soften the bad impression.

"Come. Let's come here. Here."

She leads me into a small room, very cosy, and points to the writing table.

"There. I made it for you. You'll work here. Come every day and bring your work with you. They only disturb you there at home.... Will you work here? Would you like to?"

In order not to hurt her by refusing, I answer that I shall work with her and that I like the room immensely. Then we both sit down in the cosy room and begin to talk.

The warmth, the cosy surroundings, the presence of a sympathetic being, rouses in me now not a feeling of pleasure as it used but a strong desire to complain and grumble. Anyhow it seems to me that if I moan and complain I shall feel better.

"It's a bad business, my dear," I begin with a sigh. "Very bad."

"What is the matter?"

"I'll tell you what is the matter. The best and most sacred right of kings is the right to pardon. And I have always felt myself a king so long as I used this right prodigally. I never judged, I was compassionate, I pardoned everyone right and left. Where others protested and revolted I only advised and persuaded. All my life I've tried to make my society tolerable to the family of students, friends and servants. And this attitude of mine towards people, I know, educated every one who came into contact with me. But now I am king no more. There's something going on in me which belongs only to slaves. Day and night evil thoughts roam about in my head, and feelings which I never knew before have made their home in my soul. I hate and despise; I'm exasperated, disturbed, and afraid. I've become strict beyond measure, exacting, unkind, and suspicious. Even the things which in the past gave me the chance of making an extra pun, now bring me a feeling of oppression. My logic has changed too. I used to despise money alone; now I cherish evil feelings, not to money, but to the rich, as if they were guilty. I used to hate violence and arbitrariness; now I hate the people who employ violence, as if they alone are to blame and not all of us, who cannot educate one another. What does it all mean? If my new thoughts and feelings come from a change of my convictions, where could the change have come from? Has the world grown worse and I better, or was I blind and indifferent before? But if the change is due to the general decline of my physical and mental powers—I am sick and losing weight every day—then I'm in a pitiable position. It means that my new thoughts are abnormal and unhealthy, that I must be ashamed of them and consider them valueless...."

"Sickness hasn't anything to do with it," Katy interrupts. "Your eyes are opened—that's all. You've begun to notice things you didn't want to notice before for some reason. My opinion is that you must break with your family finally first of all and then go away."

"You're talking nonsense."

"You don't love them any more. Then, why do you behave unfairly? And is it a family! Mere nobodies. If they died to-day, no one would notice their absence to-morrow."

Katy despises my wife and daughter as much as they hate her. It's scarcely possible nowadays to speak of the right of people to despise one another. But if you accept Katy's point of view and own that such a right exists, you will notice that she has the same right to despise my wife and Liza as they have to hate her.

"Mere nobodies!" she repeats. "Did you have any dinner to-day? It's a wonder they didn't forget to tell you dinner was ready. I don't know how they still remember that you exist."

"Katy!" I say sternly. "Please be quiet."

"You don't think it's fun for me to talk about them, do you? I wish I didn't know them at all. You listen to me, dear. Leave everything and go away: go abroad—the quicker, the better."

"What nonsense! What about the University?"

"And the University, too. What is it to you? There's no sense in it all. You've been lecturing for thirty years, and where are your pupils? Have you many famous scholars? Count them up. But to increase the number of doctors who exploit the general ignorance and make hundreds of thousands,—there's no need to be a good and gifted man. You aren't wanted."

"My God, how bitter you are!" I get terrified. "How bitter you are. Be quiet, or I'll go away. I can't reply to the bitter things you say."

The maid enters and calls us to tea. Thank God, our conversation changes round the samovar. I have made my moan, and now I want to indulge another senile weakness—reminiscences. I tell Katy about my past, to my great surprise with details that I never suspected I had kept safe in my memory. And she listens to me with emotion, with pride, holding her breath. I like particularly to tell how I once was a student at a seminary and how I dreamed of entering the University.

"I used to walk in the seminary garden," I tell her, "and the wind would bring the sound of a song and the thrumming of an accordion from a distant tavern, or a troika with bells would pass quickly by the seminary fence. That would be quite enough to fill not only my breast with a sense of happiness, but my stomach, legs, and hands. As I heard the sound of the accordion or the bells fading away, I would see myself a doctor and paint pictures, one more glorious than another. And, you see, my dreams came true. There were more things I dared to dream of. I have been a favourite professor thirty years, I have had excellent friends and an honourable reputation. I loved and married when I was passionately in love. I had children. Altogether, when I look back the whole of my life seems like a nice, clever composition. The only thing I have to do now is not to spoil the finale. For this, I must die like a man. If death is really a danger then I must meet it as becomes a teacher, a scholar, and a citizen of a Christian State. But I am spoiling the finale. I am drowning, and I run to you and beg for help, and you say: 'Drown. It's your duty.'"

At this point a ring at the bell sounds in the hall. Katy and I both recognise it and say:

"That must be Mikhail Fiodorovich."

And indeed in a minute Mikhail Fiodorovich, my colleague, the philologist, enters. He is a tall, well-built man about fifty years old, clean shaven, with thick grey hair and black eyebrows. He is a good man and an admirable friend. He belongs to an old aristocratic family, a prosperous and gifted house which has played a notable rôle in the history of our literature and education. He himself is clever, gifted, and highly educated, but not without his eccentricities. To a certain extent we are all eccentric, queer fellows, but his eccentricities have an element of the exceptional, not quite safe for his friends. Among the latter I know not a few who cannot see his many merits clearly because of his eccentricities.

As he walks in he slowly removes his gloves and says in his velvety bass:

"How do you do? Drinking tea. Just in time. It's hellishly cold."

Then he sits down at the table, takes a glass of tea and immediately begins to talk. What chiefly marks his way of talking is his invariably ironical tone, a mixture of philosophy and jest, like Shakespeare's grave-diggers. He always talks of serious matters; but never seriously. His opinions are always acid and provocative, but thanks to his tender, easy, jesting tone, it somehow happens that his acidity and provocativeness don't tire one's ears, and one very soon gets used to it. Every evening he brings along some half-dozen stories of the university life and generally begins with them when he sits down at the table.

"O Lord," he sighs with an amusing movement of his black eyebrows, "there are some funny people in the world."

"Who?" asks Katy.

"I was coming down after my lecture to-day and I met that old idiot N—— on the stairs. He walks along, as usual pushing out that horse jowl of his, looking for some one to bewail his headaches, his wife, and his students, who won't come to his lectures. 'Well,' I think to myself, 'he's seen me. It's all up—no hope for And so on in the same strain. Or he begins like this,

"Yesterday I was at Z's public lecture. Tell it not in Gath, but I do wonder how our alma mater dares to show the public such an ass, such a double-dyed blockhead as Z. Why he's a European fool. Good Lord, you won't find one like him in all Europe—not even if you looked in daytime, and with a lantern. Imagine it: he lectures as though he were sucking a stick of barley-sugar—su—su—su. He gets a fright because he can't make out his manuscript. His little thoughts will only just keep moving, hardly moving, like a bishop riding a bicycle. Above all you can't make out a word he says. The flies die of boredom, it's so terrific. It can only be compared with the boredom in the great Hall at the Commemoration, when the traditional speech is made. To hell with it!"

Immediately an abrupt change of subject.

"I had to make the speech; three years ago. Nicolai Stiepanovich will remember. It was hot, close. My full uniform was tight under my arms, tight as death. I read for half an hour, an hour, an hour and a half, two hours. 'Well,' I thought, 'thank God I've only ten pages left.' And I had four pages of peroration that I needn't read at all. 'Only six pages then,' I thought. Imagine it. I just gave a glance in front of me and saw sitting next to each other in the front row a general with a broad ribbon and a bishop. The poor devils were bored stiff. They were staring about madly to stop themselves from going to sleep. For all that they are still trying to look attentive, to make some appearance of understanding what I'm reading, and look as though they like it. 'Well,' I thought, 'if you like it, then you shall have it. I'll spite you.' So I set to and read the four pages, every word."

When he speaks only his eyes and eyebrows smile as it is generally with the ironical. At such moments there is no hatred or malice in his eyes but a great deal of acuteness and that peculiar fox-cunning which you can catch only in very observant people. Further, about his eyes I have noticed one more peculiarity. When he takes his glass from Katy, or listens to her remarks, or follows her with a glance as she goes out of the room for a little while, then I catch in his look something humble, prayerful, pure....

The maid takes the samovar away and puts on the table a big piece of cheese, some fruit, and a bottle of Crimean champagne, a thoroughly bad wine which Katy got to like when she lived in the Crimea. Mikhail Fiodorovich takes two packs of cards from the shelves and sets them out for patience. If one may believe his assurances, some games of patience demand a great power of combination and concentration. Nevertheless while he sets out the cards he amuses himself by talking continually. Katy follows his cards carefully, helping him more by mimicry than words. In the whole evening she drinks no more than two small glasses of wine, I drink only a quarter of a glass, the remainder of the bottle falls to Mikhail Fiodorovich, who can drink any amount without ever getting drunk.

During patience we solve all kinds of questions, mostly of the lofty order, and our dearest love, science, comes off second best.

"Science, thank God, has had her day," says Mikhail Fiodorovich very slowly. "She has had her swan-song. Ye-es. Mankind has begun to feel the desire to replace her by something else. She was grown from the soil of prejudice, fed by prejudices, and is now the same quintessence of prejudices as were her bygone grandmothers: alchemy, metaphysics and philosophy. As between European scholars and the Chinese who have no sciences at all the difference is merely trifling, a matter only of externals. The Chinese had no scientific knowledge, but what have they lost by that?"

"Flies haven't any scientific knowledge either," I say; "but what does that prove?"

"It's no use getting angry, Nicolai Stiepanich. I say this only between ourselves. I'm more cautious than you think. I shan't proclaim it from the housetops, God forbid! The masses still keep alive a prejudice that science and art are superior to agriculture and commerce, superior to crafts. Our persuasion makes a living from this prejudice. It's not for you and me to destroy it. God forbid!"

During patience the younger generation also comes in for it.

"Our public is degenerate nowadays," Mikhail Fiodorovich sighs. "I don't speak of ideals and such things, I only ask that they should be able to work and think decently. 'Sadly I look at the men of our time'—it's quite true in this connection."

"Yes, they're frightfully degenerate," Katy agrees. "Tell me, had you one single eminent person under you during the last five or ten years?"

"I don't know how it is with the other professors,—but somehow I don't recollect that it ever happened to me."

"In my lifetime I've seen a great many of your students and young scholars, a great many actors.... What happened? I never once had the luck to meet, not a hero or a man of talent, but an ordinarily interesting person. Everything's dull and incapable, swollen and pretentious...."

All these conversations about degeneracy give me always the impression that I have unwittingly overheard an unpleasant conversation about my daughter. I feel offended because the indictments are made wholesale and are based upon such ancient hackneyed commonplaces and such penny-dreadful notions as degeneracy, lack of ideals, or comparisons with the glorious past. Any indictment, even if it's made in a company of ladies, should be formulated with all possible precision; otherwise it isn't an indictment, but an empty calumny, unworthy of decent people.

I am an old man, and have served for the last thirty years; but I don't see any sign either of degeneracy or the lack of ideals. I don't find it any worse now than before. My porter, Nicolas, whose experience in this case has its value, says that students nowadays are neither better nor worse than their predecessors.

If I were asked what was the thing I did not like about my present pupils, I wouldn't say offhand or answer at length, but with a certain precision. I know their defects and there's no need for me to take refuge in a mist of commonplaces. I don't like the way they smoke, and drink spirits, and marry late; or the way they are careless and indifferent to the point of allowing students to go hungry in their midst, and not paying their debts into "The Students' Aid Society." They are ignorant of modern languages and express themselves incorrectly in Russian. Only yesterday my colleague, the hygienist, complained to me that he had to lecture twice as often because of their incompetent knowledge of physics and their complete ignorance of meteorology. They are readily influenced by the most modern writers, and some of those not the best, but they are absolutely indifferent to classics like Shakespeare, Marcus Aurelius, Epictetus and Pascal; and their worldly unpracticality shows itself mostly in their inability to distinguish between great and small. They solve all difficult questions which have a more or less social character (emigration, for instance) by getting up subscriptions, but not by the method of scientific investigation and experiment, though this is at their full disposal, and, above all, corresponds to their vocation. They readily become house-doctors, assistant house-doctors, clinical assistants, or consulting doctors, and they are prepared to keep these positions until they are forty, though independence, a sense of freedom, and personal initiative are quite as necessary in science, as, for instance, in art or commerce. I have pupils and listeners, but I have no helpers or successors. Therefore I love them and am concerned for them, but I'm not proud of them ... and so on.

However great the number of such defects may be, it's only in a cowardly and timid person that they give rise to pessimism and distraction. All of them are by nature accidental and transitory, and are completely dependent on the conditions of life. Ten years will be enough for them to disappear or give place to new and different defects, which are quite indispensable, but will in their turn give the timid a fright. Students' shortcomings often annoy me, but the annoyance is nothing in comparison with the joy I have had these thirty years in speaking with my pupils, lecturing to them, studying their relations and comparing them with people of a different class.

Mikhail Fiodorovich is a slanderer. Katy listens and neither of them notices how deep is the pit into which they are drawn by such an outwardly innocuous recreation as condemning one's neighbours. They don't realise how a simple conversation gradually turns into mockery and derision, or how they both begin even to employ the manners of calumny.

"There are some queer types to be found," says Mikhail Fiodorovich. "Yesterday I went to see our friend Yegor Pietrovich. There I found a student, one of your medicos, a third-year man, I think. His face ... rather in the style of Dobroliubov—the stamp of profound thought on his brow. We began to talk. 'My dear fellow—an extraordinary business. I've just read that some German or other—can't remember his name—has extracted a new alkaloid from the human brain—idiotine.' Do you know he really believed it, and produced an expression of respect on his face, as much as to say, 'See, what a power we are.'"

"The other day I went to the theatre. I sat down. Just in front of me in the next row two people were sitting: one, 'one of the chosen,' evidently a law student, the other a whiskery medico. The medico was as drunk as a cobbler. Not an atom of attention to the stage. Dozing and nodding. But the moment some actor began to deliver a loud monologue, or just raised his voice, my medico thrills, digs his neighbour in the ribs. 'What's he say? Something noble?' 'Noble,' answers 'the chosen.'

"'Brrravo!' bawls the medico. 'No—ble. Bravo.' You see the drunken blockhead didn't come to the theatre for art, but for something noble. He wants nobility."

Katy listens and laughs. Her laugh is rather strange. She breathes out in swift, rhythmic, and regular alternation with her inward breathing. It's as though she were playing an accordion. Of her face, only her nostrils laugh. My heart fails me. I don't know what to say. I lose my temper, crimson, jump up from my seat and cry:

"Be quiet, won't you? Why do you sit here like two toads, poisoning the air with your breath? I've had enough."

In vain I wait for them to stop their slanders. I prepare to go home. And it's time, too. Past ten o'clock.

"I'll sit here a little longer," says Mikhail Fiodorovich, "if you give me leave, Ekaterina Vladimirovna?"

"You have my leave," Katy answers.

"Bene. In that case, order another bottle, please."

Together they escort me to the hall with candles in their hands. While I'm putting on my overcoat, Mikhail Fiodorovich says:

"You've grown terribly thin and old lately. Nicolai Stiepanovich. What's the matter with you? Ill?

"Yes, a little."

"And he will not look after himself," Katy puts in sternly.

"Why don't you look after yourself? How can you go on like this? God helps those who help themselves, my dear man. Give my regards to your family and make my excuses for not coming. One of these days, before I go abroad, I'll come to say good-bye. Without fail. I'm off next week."

I came away from Katy's irritated, frightened by the talk about my illness and discontented with myself. "And why," I ask myself, "shouldn't I be attended by one of my colleagues?" Instantly I see how my friend, after sounding me, will go to the window silently, think a little while, turn towards me and say, indifferently, trying to prevent me from reading the truth in his face: "At the moment I don't see anything particular; but still, cher confrère, I would advise you to break off your work...." And that will take my last hope away.

Who doesn't have hopes? Nowadays, when I diagnose and treat myself, I sometimes hope that my ignorance deceives me, that I am mistaken about the albumen and sugar which I find, as well as about my heart, and also about the anasarca which I have noticed twice in the morning. While I read over the therapeutic text-books again with the eagerness of a hypochondriac, and change the prescriptions every day, I still believe that I will come across something hopeful. How trivial it all is!

Whether the sky is cloudy all over or the moon and stars are shining in it, every time I come back home I look at it and think that death will take me soon. Surely at that moment my thoughts should be as deep as the sky, as bright, as striking ... but no! I think of myself, of my wife, Liza, Gnekker, the students, people in general. My thoughts are not good, they are mean; I juggle with myself, and at this moment my attitude towards life can be expressed in the words the famous Arakheev wrote in one of his intimate letters: "All good in the world is inseparably linked to bad, and there is always more bad than good." Which means that everything is ugly, there's nothing to live for, and the sixty-two years I have lived out must be counted as lost. I surprise myself in these thoughts and try to convince myself they are accidental and temporary and not deeply rooted in me, but I think immediately:

"If that's true, why am I drawn every evening to those two toads." And I swear to myself never to go to Katy any more, though I know I will go to her again to-morrow.

As I pull my door bell and go upstairs, I feel already that I have no family and no desire to return to it. It is plain my new, Arakheev thoughts are not accidental or temporary in me, but possess my whole being. With a bad conscience, dull, indolent, hardly able to move my limbs, as though I had a ten ton weight upon me, I lie down in my bed and soon fall asleep.

And then—insomnia.

IV

The summer comes and life changes.

One fine morning Liza comes in to me and says in a joking tone:

"Come, Your Excellency. It's all ready."

They lead My Excellency into the street, put me into a cab and drive me away. For want of occupation I read the signboards backwards as I go. The word "Tavern" becomes "Nrevat." That would do for a baron's name: Baroness Nrevat. Beyond, I drive across the field by the cemetery, which produces no impression upon me whatever, though I'll soon lie there. After a two hours' drive, My Excellency is led into the ground-floor of the bungalow, and put into a small, lively room with a light-blue paper.

Insomnia at night as before, but I am no more wakeful in the morning and don't listen to my wife, but lie in bed. I don't sleep, but I am in a sleepy state, half-forgetfulness, when you know you are not asleep, but have dreams. I get up in the afternoon, and sit down at the table by force of habit, but now I don't work any more but amuse myself with French yellow-backs sent me by Katy. Of course it would be more patriotic to read Russian authors, but to tell the truth I'm not particularly disposed to them. Leaving out two or three old ones, all the modern literature doesn't seem to me to be literature but a unique home industry which exists only to be encouraged, but the goods are bought with reluctance. The best of these homemade goods can't be called remarkable and it's impossible to praise it sincerely without a saving "but"; and the same must be said of all the literary novelties I've read during the last ten or fifteen years. Not one remarkable, and you can't dispense with "but." They have cleverness, nobility, and no talent; talent, nobility and no cleverness; or finally, talent, cleverness, but no nobility.

I would not say that French books have talent, cleverness, and nobility. Nor do they satisfy me. But they are not so boring as the Russian; and it is not rare to find in them the chief constituent of creative genius—the sense of personal freedom, which is lacking to Russian authors. I do not recall one single new book in which from the very first page the author did not try to tie himself up in all manner of conventions and contracts with his conscience. One is frightened to speak of the naked body, another is bound hand and foot by psychological analysis, a third must have "a kindly attitude to his fellow-men," the fourth heaps up whole pages with descriptions of nature on purpose to avoid any suspicion of a tendency.... One desires to be in his books a bourgeois at all costs, another at all costs an aristocrat. Deliberation, cautiousness, cunning: but no freedom, no courage to write as one likes, and therefore no creative genius.

All this refers to belles-lettres, so-called.

As for serious articles in Russian, on sociology, for instance, or art and so forth, I don't read them, simply out of timidity. For some reason in my childhood and youth I had a fear of porters and theatre attendants, and this fear has remained with me up till now. Even now I am afraid of them. It is said that only that which one cannot understand seems terrible. And indeed it is very difficult to understand why hall-porters and theatre attendants are so pompous and haughty and importantly polite. When I read serious articles, I have exactly the same indefinable fear. Their portentous gravity, their playfulness, like an archbishop's, their over-familiar attitude to foreign authors, their capacity for talking dignified nonsense—"filling a vacuum with emptiness"—it is all inconceivable to me and terrifying, and quite unlike the modesty and the calm and gentlemanly tone to which I am accustomed when reading our writers on medicine and the natural sciences. Not only articles; I have difficulty also in reading translations even when they are edited by serious Russians. The presumptuous benevolence of the prefaces, the abundance of notes by the translator (which prevents one from concentrating), the parenthetical queries and sics, which are so liberally scattered over the book or the article by the translator—seem to me an assault on the author's person, as well as on my independence as a reader.

Once I was invited as an expert to the High Court. In the interval one of my fellow-experts called my attention to the rude behaviour of the public prosecutor to the prisoners, among whom were two women intellectuals. I don't think I exaggerated at all when I replied to my colleague that he was not behaving more rudely than authors of serious articles behave to one another. Indeed their behaviour is so rude that one speaks of them with bitterness. They behave to each other or to the writers whom they criticise either with too much deference, careless of their own dignity, or, on the other hand, they treat them much worse than I have treated Gnekker, my future son-in-law, in these notes and thoughts of mine. Accusations of irresponsibility, of impure intentions, of any kind of crime even, are the usual adornment of serious articles. And this, as our young medicos love to say in their little articles—quite ultima ratio. Such an attitude must necessarily be reflected in the character of the young generation of writers, and therefore I'm not at all surprised that in the new books which, have been added to our belles lettres in the last ten or fifteen years, the heroes drink a great deal of vodka and the heroines are not sufficiently chaste.

I read French books and look out of the window, which is open—I see the pointed palings of my little garden, two or three skinny trees, and there, beyond the garden, the road, fields, then a wide strip of young pine-forest. I often delight in watching a little boy and girl, both white-haired and ragged, climb on the garden fence and laugh at my baldness. In their shining little eyes I read, "Come out, thou bald-head." These are almost the only people who don't care a bit about my reputation or my title.

I don't have visitors everyday now. I'll mention only the visits of Nicolas and Piotr Ignatievich. Nicolas comes to me usually on holidays, pretending to come on business, but really to see me. He is very hilarious, a thing which never happens to him in the winter.

"Well, what have you got to say?" I ask him, coming out into the passage.

"Your Excellency!" he says, pressing his hand to his heart and looking at me with a lover's rapture. "Your Excellency! So help me God! God strike me where I stand! Gaudeamus igitur juvenestus."

And he kisses me eagerly on the shoulders, on my sleeves, and buttons.

"Is everything all right over there?" I ask.

"Your Excellency! I swear to God...."

He never stops swearing, quite unnecessarily, and I soon get bored, and send him to the kitchen, where they give him dinner. Piotr Ignatievich also comes on holidays specially to visit me and communicate his thoughts to me. He usually sits by the table in my room, modest, clean, judicious, without daring to cross his legs or lean his elbows on the table, all the while telling me in a quiet, even voice what he considers very piquant items of news gathered from journals and pamphlets.

These items are all alike and can be reduced to the following type: A Frenchman made a discovery. Another—a German—exposed him by showing that this discovery had been made as long ago as 1870 by some American. Then a third—also a German—outwitted them both by showing that both of them had been confused, by taking spherules of air under a microscope for dark pigment. Even when he wants to make me laugh, Piotr Ignatievich tells his story at great length, very much as though he were defending a thesis, enumerating his literary sources in detail, with every effort to avoid mistakes in the dates, the particular number of the journal and the names. Moreover, he does not say Petit simply but inevitably, Jean Jacques Petit. If he happens to stay to dinner, he will tell the same sort of piquant stories and drive all the company to despondency. If Gnekker and Liza begin to speak of fugues and counter-fugues in his presence he modestly lowers his eyes, and his face falls. He is ashamed that such trivialities should be spoken of in the presence of such serious men as him and me.

In my present state of mind five minutes are enough for him to bore me as though I had seen and listened to him for a whole eternity. I hate the poor man. I wither away beneath his quiet, even voice and his bookish language. His stories make me stupid.... He cherishes the kindliest feelings towards me and talks to me only to give me pleasure. I reward him by staring at his face as if I wanted to hypnotise him, and thinking "Go away. Go, go...." But he is proof against my mental suggestion and sits, sits, sits....

While he sits with me I cannot rid myself of the idea: "When I die, it's quite possible that he will be appointed in my place." Then my poor audience appears to me as an oasis where the stream has dried, up, and I am unkind to Piotr Ignatievich, and silent and morose as if he were guilty of such thoughts and not I myself. When he begins, as usual, to glorify the German scholars, I no longer jest good-naturedly, but murmur sternly:

"They're fools, your Germans...."

It's like the late Professor Nikita Krylov when he was bathing with Pirogov at Reval. He got angry with the water, which was very cold, and swore about "These scoundrelly Germans." I behave badly to Piotr Ignatievich; and it's only when he is going away and I see through the window his grey hat disappearing behind the garden fence, that I want to call him back and say: "Forgive me, my dear fellow."

The dinner goes yet more wearily than in winter. The same Gnekker, whom I now hate and despise, dines with me every day. Before, I used to suffer his presence in silence, but now I say biting things to him, which make my wife and Liza blush. Carried away by an evil feeling, I often say things that are merely foolish, end don't know why I say them. Thus it happened once that after looking at Gnekker contemptuously for a long while, I suddenly fired off, for no reason at all:

"Eagles than barnyard-fowls may lower bend;

But fowls shall never to the heav'ns ascend."

More's the pity that the fowl Gnekker shows himself more clever than the eagle professor. Knowing my wife and daughter are on his side he maintains these tactics. He replies to my shafts with a condescending silence ("The old man's off his head.... What's the good of talking to him?"), or makes good-humoured fun of me. It is amazing to what depths of pettiness a man may descend. During the whole dinner I can dream how Gnekker will be shown to be an adventurer, how Liza and my wife will realise their mistake, and I will tease them—ridiculous dreams like these at a time when I have one foot in the grave.

Now there occur misunderstandings, of a kind which I formerly knew only by hearsay. Though it is painful I will describe one which occurred after dinner the other day. I sit in my room smoking a little pipe. Enters my wife, as usual, sits down and begins to talk. What a good idea it would be to go to Kharkov now while the weather is warm and there is the time, and inquire what kind of man our Gnekker is.

"Very well. I'll go," I agree.

My wife gets up, pleased with me, and walks to the door; but immediately returns:

"By-the bye, I've one more favour to ask. I know you'll be angry; but it's my duty to warn you.... Forgive me, Nicolai,—but all our neighbours have begun to talk about the way you go to Katy's continually. I don't deny that she's clever and educated. It's pleasant to spend the time with her. But at your age and in your position it's rather strange to find pleasure in her society.... Besides she has a reputation enough to...."

All my blood rushes instantly from my brain. My eyes flash fire. I catch hold of my hair, and stamp and cry, in a voice that is not mine:

"Leave me alone, leave me, leave me...."

My face is probably terrible, and my voice strange, for my wife suddenly gets pale, and calls aloud, with a despairing voice, also not her own. At our cries rush in Liza and Gnekker, then Yegor.

My feet grow numb, as though they did not exist. I feel that I am falling into somebody's arms. Then I hear crying for a little while and sink into a faint which lasts for two or three hours.

Now for Katy. She comes to see me before evening every day, which of course must be noticed by my neighbours and my friends. After a minute she takes me with her for a drive. She has her own horse and a new buggy she bought this summer. Generally she lives like a princess. She has taken an expensive detached bungalow with a big garden, and put into it all her town furniture. She has two maids and a coachman. I often ask her:

"Katy, what will you live on when you've spent all your father's money?"

"We'll see, then," she answers.

"But this money deserves to be treated more seriously, my dear. It was earned by a good man and honest labour."

"You've told me that before. I know."

First we drive by the field, then by a young pine forest, which you can see from my window. Nature seems to me as beautiful as she used, although the devil whispers to me that all these pines and firs, the birds and white clouds in the sky will not notice my absence in three or four months when I am dead. Katy likes to take the reins, and it is good that the weather is fine and I am sitting by her side. She is in a happy mood, and does not say bitter things.

"You're a very good man, Nicolai," she says. "You are a rare bird. There's no actor who could play your part. Mine or Mikhail's, for instance—even a bad actor could manage, but yours—there's nobody. I envy you, envy you terribly I What am I? What?"

She thinks for a moment, and asks:

"I'm a negative phenomenon, aren't I?"

"Yes," I answer.

"H'm ... what's to be done then?"

What answer can I give? It's easy to say "Work," or "Give your property to the poor," or "Know yourself," and because it's so easy to say this I don't know what to answer.

My therapeutist colleagues, when teaching methods of cure, advise one "to individualise each particular case." This advice must be followed in order to convince one's self that the remedies recommended in the text-books as the best and most thoroughly suitable as a general rule, are quite unsuitable in particular cases. It applies to moral affections as well. But I must answer something. So I say:

"You've too much time on your hands, my dear. You must take up something.... In fact, why shouldn't you go on the stage again, if you have a vocation."

"I can't."

"You have the manner and tone of a victim. I don't like it, my dear. You have yourself to blame. Remember, you began by getting angry with people and things in general; but you never did anything to improve either of them. You didn't put up a struggle against the evil. You got tired. You're not a victim of the struggle but of your own weakness. Certainly you were young then and inexperienced. But now everything can be different. Come on, be an actress. You will work; you will serve in the temple of art."...

"Don't be so clever, Nicolai," she interrupts. "Let's agree once for all: let's speak about actors, actresses, writers, but let us leave art out of it. You're a rare and excellent man. But you don't understand enough about art to consider it truly sacred. You have no flair, no ear for art. You've been busy all your life, and you never had time to acquire the flair. Really ... I don't love these conversations about art!" she continues nervously. "I don't love them. They've vulgarised it enough already, thank you."

"Who's vulgarised it?"

"They vulgarised it by their drunkenness, newspapers by their over-familiarity, clever people by philosophy."

"What's philosophy got to do with it?"

"A great deal. If a man philosophises, it means he doesn't understand."

So that it should not come to bitter words, I hasten to change the subject, and then keep silence for a long while. It's not till we come out of the forest and drive towards Katy's bungalow, I return to the subject and ask:

"Still, you haven't answered me why you don't want to go on the stage?"

"Really, it's cruel," she cries out, and suddenly blushes all over. "You want me to tell you the truth outright. Very well if ... if you will have it I I've no talent! No talent and ... much ambition! There you are!"

After this confession, she turns her face away from me, and to hide the trembling of her hands, tugs at the reins.

As we approach her bungalow, from a distance we see Mikhail already, walking about by the gate, impatiently awaiting us.

"This Fiodorovich again," Katy says with annoyance. "Please take him away from me. I'm sick of him. He's flat.... Let him go to the deuce."

Mikhail Fiodorovich ought to have gone abroad long ago, but he has postponed his departure every week. There have been some changes in him lately. He's suddenly got thin, begun to be affected by drink—a thing that never happened to him before, and his black eyebrows have begun to get grey. When our buggy stops at the gate he cannot hide his joy and impatience. Anxiously he helps Katy and me from the buggy, hastily asks us questions, laughs, slowly rubs his hands, and that gentle, prayerful, pure something that I used to notice only in his eyes is now poured over all his face. He is happy and at the same time ashamed of his happiness, ashamed of his habit of coming to Katy's every evening, and he finds it necessary to give a reason for his coming, some obvious absurdity, like: "I was passing on business, and I thought I'd just drop in for a second."

All three of us go indoors. First we drink tea, then our old friends, the two packs of cards, appear on the table, with a big piece of cheese, some fruit, and a bottle of Crimean champagne. The subjects of conversation are not new, but all exactly the same as they were in the winter. The university, the students, literature, the theatre—all of them come in for it. The air thickens with slanders, and grows more dose. It is poisoned by the breath, not of two toads as in winter, but now by all three. Besides the velvety, baritone laughter and the accordion-like giggle, the maid who waits upon us hears also the unpleasant jarring laugh of a musical comedy general: "He, he, he!"

V

There sometimes come fearful nights with thunder, lightning, rain, and wind, which the peasants call "sparrow-nights." There was one such sparrow-night in my own personal life....

I wake after midnight and suddenly leap out of bed. Somehow it seems to me that I am going to die immediately. I do not know why, for there is no single sensation in my body which points to a quick end; but a terror presses on my soul as though I had suddenly seen a huge, ill-boding fire in the sky.

I light the lamp quickly and drink some water straight out of the decanter. Then I hurry to the window. The weather is magnificent. The air smells of hay and some delicious thing besides. I see the spikes of my garden fence, the sleepy starveling trees by the window, the road, the dark strip of forest. There is a calm and brilliant moon in the sky and not a single cloud. Serenity. Not a leaf stirs. To me it seems that everything is looking at me and listening for me to die.

Dread seizes me. I shut the window and run to the bed, I feel for my pulse. I cannot find it in my wrist; I seek it in my temples, my chin, my hand again. They are all cold and slippery with sweat. My breathing comes quicker and quicker; my body trembles, all my bowels are stirred, and my face and forehead feel as though a cobweb had settled on them.

What shall I do? Shall I call my family? No use. I do not know what my wife and Liza will do when they come in to me.

I hide my head under the pillow, shut my eyes and wait, wait.... My spine is cold. It almost contracts within me. And I feel that death will approach me only from behind, very quietly.

"Kivi, kivi." A squeak sounds in the stillness of the night. I do not know whether it is in my heart or in the street.

God, how awful! I would drink some more water; but now I dread opening my eyes, and fear to raise my head. The terror is unaccountable, animal. I cannot understand why I am afraid. Is it because I want to live, or because a new and unknown pain awaits me?

Upstairs, above the ceiling, a moan, then a laugh ... I listen. A little after steps sound on the staircase. Someone hurries down, then up again. In a minute steps sound downstairs again. Someone stops by my door and listens.

"Who's there?" I call.

The door opens. I open my eyes boldly and see my wife. Her face is pale and her eyes red with weeping.

"You're not asleep, Nicolai Stiepanovich?" she asks.

"What is it?"

"For God's sake go down to Liza. Something is wrong with her."

"Very well ... with pleasure," I murmur, very glad that I am not alone. "Very well ... immediately."

As I follow my wife I hear what she tells me, and from agitation understand not a word. Bright spots from her candle dance over the steps of the stairs; our long shadows tremble; my feet catch in the skirts of my dressing-gown. My breath goes, and it seems to me that someone is chasing me, trying to seize my back. "I shall die here on the staircase, this second," I think, "this second." But we have passed the staircase, the dark hall with the Italian window and we go into Liza's room. She sits in bed in her chemise; her bare legs hang down and she moans.

"Oh, my God ... oh, my God!" she murmurs, half shutting her eyes from our candles. "I can't, I can't."

"Liza, my child," I say, "what's the matter?"

Seeing me, she calls out and falls on my neck.

"Papa darling," she sobs. "Papa dearest ... my sweet. I don't know what it is.... It hurts."

She embraces me, kisses me and lisps endearments which I heard her lisp when she was still a baby.

"Be calm, my child. God's with you," I say. "You mustn't cry. Something hurts me too."

I try to cover her with the bedclothes; my wife gives her to drink; and both of us jostle in confusion round the bed. My shoulders push into hers, and at that moment I remember how we used to bathe our children.

"But help her, help her!" my wife implores. "Do something!" And what can I do? Nothing. There is some weight on the girl's soul; but I understand nothing, know nothing and can only murmur:

"It's nothing, nothing.... It will pass.... Sleep, sleep."

As if on purpose a dog suddenly howls in the yard, at first low and irresolute, then aloud, in two voices. I never put any value on such signs as dogs' whining or screeching owls; but now my heart contracts painfully, and I hasten to explain the howling.

"Nonsense," I think. "It's the influence of one organism on another. My great nervous strain was transmitted to my wife, to Liza, and to the dog. That's all. Such transmissions explain presentiments and previsions."

A little later when I return to my room to write a prescription for Liza I no longer think that I shall die soon. My soul simply feels heavy and dull, so that I am even sad that I did not die suddenly. For a long while I stand motionless in the middle of the room, pondering what I shall prescribe for Liza; but the moans above the ceiling are silent and I decide not to write a prescription, but stand there still.

There is a dead silence, a silence, as one man wrote, that rings in one's ears. The time goes slowly. The bars of moonshine on the windowsill do not move from their place, as though congealed.... The dawn is still far away.

But the garden-gate creaks; someone steals in, and strips a twig from the starveling trees, and cautiously knocks with it on my window.

"Nicolai Stiepanovich!" I hear a whisper. "Nicolai Stiepanovich!"

I open the window, and I think that I am dreaming. Under the window, close against the wall stands a woman in a blade dress. She is brightly lighted by the moon and looks at me with wide eyes. Her face is pale, stem and fantastic in the moon, like marble. Her chin trembles.

"It is I...." she says, "I ... Katy!"

In the moon all women's eyes are big and black, people are taller and paler. Probably that is the reason why I did not recognise her in the first moment.

"What's the matter?"

"Forgive me," she says. "I suddenly felt so dreary ... I could not bear it. So I came here. There's a light in your window ... and I decided to knock.... Forgive me.... Ah, if you knew how dreary I felt! What are you doing now?"

"Nothing. Insomnia."

Her eyebrows lift, her eyes shine with tears and all her face is illumined as with light, with the familiar, but long unseen, look of confidence.

"Nicolai Stiepanovich!" she says imploringly, stretching out both her hands to me. "Dear, I beg you ... I implore.... If you do not despise my friendship and my respect for you, then do what I implore you."

"What is it?"

"Take my money."

"What next? What's the good of your money to me?"

"You will go somewhere to be cured. You must cure yourself. You will take it? Yes? Dear ... Yes?"

She looks into my face eagerly and repeats:

"Yes? You will take it?"

"No, my dear, I won't take it....", I say. "Thank you."

She turns her back to me and lowers her head. Probably the tone of my refusal would not allow any further talk of money.

"Go home to sleep," I say. "I'll see you to-morrow."

"It means, you don't consider me your friend?" she asks sadly.

"I don't say that. But your money is no good to me."

"Forgive me," she says lowering her voice by a full octave. "I understand you. To be obliged to a person like me ... a retired actress... But good-bye."

And she walks away so quickly that I have no time even to say "Good-bye."

VI

I am in Kharkov.

Since it would be useless to fight against my present mood, and I have no power to do it, I made up my mind that the last days of my life shall be irreproachable, on the formal side. If I am not right with my family, which I certainly admit, I will try at least to do as it wishes. Besides I am lately become so indifferent that it's positively all the same, to me whether I go to Kharkov, or Paris, or Berditshev.

I arrived here at noon and put up at a hotel not far from the cathedral. The train made me giddy, the draughts blew through me, and now I am sitting on the bed with my head in my hands waiting for the tic. I ought to go to my professor friends to-day, but I have neither the will nor the strength.

The old hall-porter comes in to ask whether I have brought my own bed-clothes. I keep him about five minutes asking him questions about Gnekker, on whose account I came here. The porter happens to be Kharkov-born, and knows the town inside out; but he doesn't remember any family with the name of Gnekker. I inquire about the estate. The answer is the same.

The clock in the passage strikes one,... two,... three.... The last months of my life, while I wait for death, seem to me far longer than my whole life. Never before could I reconcile myself to the slowness of time as I can now. Before, when I had to wait for a train at the station, or to sit at an examination, a quarter of an hour would seem an eternity.

Now I can sit motionless in bed the whole night long, quite calmly thinking that there will be the same long, colourless night to-morrow, and the next day....

In the passage the clock strikes five, six, seven.... It grows dark. There is dull pain in my cheek—the beginning of the tic. To occupy myself with thoughts, I return to my old point of view, when I was not indifferent, and ask: Why do I, a famous man, a privy councillor, sit in this little room, on this bed with a strange grey blanket? Why do I look at this cheap tin washstand and listen to the wretched clock jarring in the passage? Is all this worthy of my fame and my high position among people? And I answer these questions with a smile. My naïveté seems funny to me—the naïveté with which as a young man I exaggerated the value of fame and of the exclusive position which famous men enjoy. I am famous, my name is spoken with reverence. My portrait has appeared in "Niva" and in "The Universal Illustration." I've even read my biography in a German paper, but what of that? I sit lonely, by myself, in a strange city, on a strange bed, rubbing my aching cheek with my palm....

Family scandals, the hardness of creditors, the rudeness of railway men, the discomforts of the passport system, the expensive and unwholesome food at the buffets, the general coarseness and roughness of people,—all this and a great deal more that would take too long to put down, concerns me as much as it concerns any bourgeois who is known only in his own little street. Where is the exclusiveness of my position then? We will admit that I am infinitely famous, that I am a hero of whom my country is proud. All the newspapers give bulletins of my illness, the post is already bringing in sympathetic addresses from my friends, my pupils, and the public. But all this will not save me from dying in anguish on a stranger's bed in utter loneliness. Of course there is no one to blame for this. But I must confess I do not like my popularity. I feel that it has deceived me.

At about ten I fall asleep, and, in spite of the tic sleep soundly, and would sleep for a long while were I not awakened. Just after one there is a sudden knock on my door.

"Who's there?"

"A telegram."

"You could have brought it to-morrow," I storm, as I take the telegram from the porter. "Now I shan't sleep again."

"I'm sorry. There was a light in your room. I thought you were not asleep."

I open the telegram and look first at the signature—my wife's. What does she want?

"Gnekker married Liza secretly yesterday. Return."

I read the telegram. For a long while I am not startled. Not Gnekker's or Liza's action frightens me, but the indifference with which I receive the news of their marriage. Men say that philosophers and true savants are indifferent. It is untrue. Indifference is the paralysis of the soul, premature death.

I go to bed again and begin to ponder with what thoughts I can occupy myself. What on earth shall I think of? I seem to have thought over everything, and now there is nothing powerful enough to rouse my thought.

When the day begins to dawn, I sit in bed clasping my knees and, for want of occupation I try to know myself. "Know yourself" is good, useful advice; but it is a pity that the ancients did not think of showing us the way to avail ourselves of it.

Before, when I had the desire to understand somebody else, or myself, I used not to take into consideration actions, wherein everything is conditional, but desires. Tell me what you want, and I will tell you what you are.

And now I examine myself. What do I want?

I want our wives, children, friends, and pupils to love in us, not the name or the firm or the label, but the ordinary human beings. What besides? I should like to have assistants and successors. What more? I should like to wake in a hundred years' time, and take a look, if only with one eye, at what has happened to science. I should like to live ten years more.... What further?

Nothing further. I think, think a long while and cannot make out anything else. However much I were to think, wherever my thoughts should stray, it is clear to me that the chief, all-important something is lacking in my desires. In my infatuation for science, my desire to live, my sitting here on a strange bed, my yearning to know myself, in all the thoughts, feelings, and ideas I form about anything, there is wanting the something universal which could bind all these together in one whole. Each feeling and thought lives detached in me, and in all my opinions about science, the theatre, literature, and my pupils, and in all the little pictures which my imagination paints, not even the most cunning analyst will discover what is called the general idea, or the god of the living man.

And if this is not there, then nothing is there.

In poverty such as this a serious infirmity, fear of death, influence of circumstances and people would have been enough to overthrow and shatter all that I formerly considered as my conception of the world, and all wherein I saw the meaning and joy of my life. Therefore, it is nothing strange that I have darkened the last months of my life by thoughts and feelings worthy of a slave or a savage, and that I am now indifferent and do not notice the dawn. If there is lacking in a man that which is higher and stronger than all outside influences, then verily a good cold in the head is enough to upset his balance and to make him see each bird an owl and hear a dog's whine in every sound; and all his pessimism or his optimism with their attendant thoughts, great and small, seem then to be merely symptoms and no more.

I am beaten. Then it's no good going on thinking, no good talking. I shall sit and wait in silence for what will come.

In the morning the porter brings me tea and the local paper. Mechanically I read the advertisements on the first page, the leader, the extracts from newspapers and magazines, the local news ... Among other things I find in the local news an item like this: "Our famous scholar, emeritus professor Nicolai Stiepanovich arrived in Kharkov yesterday by the express, and stayed at——hotel."

Evidently big names are created to live detached from those who bear them. Now my name walks in Kharkov undisturbed. In some three months it will shine as bright as the sun itself, inscribed in letters of gold on my tombstone—at a time when I myself will be under the sod....

A faint knock at the door. Somebody wants me.

"Who's there? Come in!"

The door opens. I step back in astonishment, and hasten to pull my dressing gown together. Before me stands Katy.

"How do you do?" she says, panting from running up the stairs. "You didn't expect me? I ... I've come too."

She sits down and continues, stammering and looking away from me. "Why don't you say 'Good morning'? I arrived too ... to-day. I found out you were at this hotel, and came to see you."

"I'm delighted to see you," I say shrugging my shoulders. "But I'm surprised. You might have dropped straight from heaven. What are you doing here?"

"I?... I just came."

Silence. Suddenly she gets up impetuously and comes over to me.

"Nicolai Stiepanich!" she says, growing pale and pressing her hands to her breast. "Nicolai Stiepanich! I can't go on like this any longer. I can't. For God's sake tell me now, immediately. What shall I do? Tell me, what shall I do?"

"What can I say? I am beaten. I can say nothing."

"But tell me, I implore you," she continues, out of breath and trembling all over her body. "I swear to you, I can't go on like this any longer. I haven't the strength."

She drops into a chair and begins to sob. She throws her head back, wrings her hands, stamps with her feet; her hat falls from her head and dangles by its string, her hair is loosened.

"Help me, help," she implores. "I can't bear it any more."

She takes a handkerchief out of her little travelling bag and with it pulls out some letters which fall from her knees to the floor. I pick them up from the floor and recognise on one of them Mikhail Fiodorovich's hand-writing, and accidentally read part of a word: "passionat...."

"There's nothing that I can say to you, Katy," I say.

"Help me," she sobs, seizing my hand and kissing it. "You're my father, my only friend. You're wise and learned, and you've lived long! You were a teacher. Tell me what to do."

I am bewildered and surprised, stirred by her sobbing, and I can hardly stand upright.

"Let's have some breakfast, Katy," I say with a constrained smile.

Instantly I add in a sinking voice:

"I shall be dead soon, Katy...."

"Only one word, only one word," she weeps and stretches out her hands to me. "What shall I do?"

"You're a queer thing, really....", I murmur. "I can't understand it. Such a clever woman and suddenly—weeping...."

Comes silence. Katy arranges her hair, puts on her hat, then crumples her letters and stuffs them in her little bag, all in silence and unhurried. Her face, her bosom and her gloves are wet with tears, but her expression is dry already, stern.... I look at her and am ashamed that I am happier than she. It was but a little while before my death, in the ebb of my life, that I noticed in myself the absence of what our friends the philosophers call the general idea; but this poor thing's soul has never known and never will know shelter all her life, all her life.

"Katy, let's have breakfast," I say.

"No, thank you," she answers coldly.

One minute more passes in silence.

"I don't like Kharkov," I say. "It's too grey. A grey city."

"Yes ... ugly.... I'm not here for long.... On my way. I leave to-day."

"For where?"

"For the Crimea ... I mean, the Caucasus."

"So. For long?"

"I don't know."

Katy gets up and gives me her hand with a cold smile, looking away from me.

I would like to ask her: "That means you won't be at my funeral?" But she does not look at me; her hand is cold and like a stranger's. I escort her to the door in silenqe.... She goes out of my room and walks down the long passage, without looking back. She knows that my eyes are following her, and probably on the landing she will look back.

No, she did not look back. The black dress showed for the last time, her steps were stilled.... Goodbye, my treasure!

THE FIT

I

The medical student Mayer, and Ribnikov, a student at the Moscow school of painting, sculpture, and architecture, came one evening to their friend Vassiliev, law student, and proposed that he should go with them to S——v Street. For a long while Vassiliev did not agree, but eventually dressed himself and went with them.

Unfortunate women he knew only by hearsay and from books, and never once in his life had he been in the houses where they live. He knew there were immoral women who were forced by the pressure of disastrous circumstances—environment, bad up-bringing, poverty, and the like—to sell their honour for money. They do not know pure love, have no children and no legal rights; mothers and sisters mourn them for dead, science treats them as an evil, men are familiar with them. But notwithstanding all this they do not lose the image and likeness of God. They all acknowledge their sin and hope for salvation. They are free to avail themselves of every means of salvation. True, Society does not forgive people their past, but with God Mary of Egypt is not lower than the other saints. Whenever Vassiliev recognised an unfortunate woman in the street by her costume or her manner, or saw a picture of one in a comic paper, there came into his mind every time a story he once read somewhere: a pure and heroic young man falls in love with an unfortunate woman and asks her to be his wife, but she, considering herself unworthy of such happiness, poisons herself.

Vassiliev lived in one of the streets off the Tverskoi boulevard. When he and his friends came out of the house it was about eleven o'clock—the first snow had just fallen and all nature was under the spell of this new snow; The air smelt of snow, the snow cracked softly under foot, the earth, the roofs, the trees, the benches on the boulevards—all were soft, white, and young. Owing to this the houses had a different look from yesterday, the lamps burned brighter, the air was more transparent, the clatter of the cabs was dulled and there entered into the soul with the fresh, easy, frosty air a feeling like the white, young, feathery snow. "To these sad shores unknowing" the medico began to sing in a pleasant tenor, "An unknown power entices...."

"Behold the mill" ... the painter's voice took him up, "it is now fall'n to ruin."

"Behold the mill, it is now fall'n to ruin," the medico repeated, raising his eyebrows and sadly shaking his head.

He was silent for a while, passed his hand over his forehead trying to recall the words, and began to sing in a loud voice and so well that the passers-by looked back.

"Here, long ago, came free, free love to me"...

All three went into a restaurant and without taking off their coats they each had two thimblefuls of vodka at the bar. Before drinking the second, Vassiliev noticed a piece of cork in his Vodka, lifted the glass to his eye, looked at it for a long while with a short-sighted frown. The medico misunderstood his expression and said—

"Well, what are you staring at? No philosophy, please. Vodka's made to be drunk, caviare to be eaten, women to sleep with, snow to walk on. Live like a man for one evening."

"Well, I've nothing to say," said Vassiliev laughingly, "I'm not refusing?"

The vodka warmed his breast. He looked at his friends, admired and envied them. How balanced everything is in these healthy, strong, cheerful people. Everything in their minds and souls is smooth and rounded off. They sing, have a passion for the theatre, paint, talk continually, and drink, and they never have a headache the next day. They are romantic and dissolute, sentimental and insolent; they can work and go on the loose and laugh at nothing and talk rubbish; they are hot-headed, honest, heroic and as human beings not a bit worse than Vassiliev, who watches his every step and word, who is careful, cautious, and able to give the smallest trifle the dignity of a problem. And he made tip his mind if only for one evening to live like his friends, to let himself go, and be free from his own control. Must he drink vodka? He'll drink, even if his head falls to pieces to-morrow. Must he be taken to women? He'll go. He'll laugh, play the fool, and give a joking answer to disapproving passers-by.

He came out of the restaurant laughing. He liked his friends—one in a battered hat with a wide brim who aped aesthetic disorder; the other in a sealskin cap, not very poor, with a pretence of learned Bohemia. He liked the snow, the paleness, the lamp-lights, the dear black prints which the passers' feet left on the snow. He liked the air, and above all the transparent, tender, naive, virgin tone which can be seen in nature only twice in the year: when everything is covered in snow, on the bright days in spring, and on moonlight nights when the ice breaks on the river.

"To these sad shores unknowing," he began to sing sotto-voce, "An unknown power entices."

And all the way for some reason or other he and his friends had this melody on their lips. All three hummed it mechanically out of time with each other.

Vassiliev Imagined how in about ten minutes he and his friends would knock at a door, how they would stealthily walk through-the narrow little passages and dark rooms to the women, how he would take advantage of the dark, suddenly strike a match, and see lit up a suffering face and a guilty smile. There he will surely find a fair or a dark woman in a white nightgown with her hair loose. She will be frightened of the light, dreadfully confused and say: "Good God! What are you doing? Blow it out!" All this was frightening, but curious and novel.

II

The friends turned out of Trubnoi Square into the Grachovka and soon arrived at the street which Vassiliev knew only from hearsay. Seeing two rows of houses with brightly lighted windows and wide open doors, and hearing the gay sound of pianos and fiddles—sounds which flew out of all the doors and mingled in a strange confusion, as if somewhere in the darkness over the roof-tops an unseen orchestra were tuning, Vassiliev was bewildered and said:

"What a lot of houses!"

"What's that?" said the medico. "There are ten times as many in London. There are a hundred thousand of these women there."

The cabmen sat on their boxes quiet and indifferent as in other streets; on the pavement walked the same passers-by. No one was in a hurry; no one hid his face in his collar; no one shook his head reproachfully. And in this indifference, in the confused sound of the pianos and fiddles, in the bright windows and wide-open doors, something very free, impudent, bold and daring could be felt. It must have been the same as this in the old times on the slave-markets, as gay and as noisy; people looked and walked with the same indifference.

"Let's begin right at the beginning," said the painter.

The friends walked into a narrow little passage lighted by a single lamp with a reflector. When they opened the door a man in a black jacket rose lazily from the yellow sofa in the hall. He had an unshaven lackey's face and sleepy eyes. The place smelt like a laundry, and of vinegar. From the hall a door led into a brightly lighted room. The medico and the painter stopped in the doorway, stretched out their necks and peeped into the room together:

"Buona sera, signore, Rigoletto—huguenote—traviata!—" the painter began, making a theatrical bow.

"Havanna—blackbeetlano—pistoletto!" said the medico, pressing his hat to his heart and bowing low.

Vassiliev kept behind them. He wanted to bow theatrically too and say something silly. But he only smiled, felt awkward and ashamed, and awaited impatiently what was to follow. In the door appeared a little fair girl of seventeen or eighteen, with short hair, wearing a short blue dress with a white bow on her breast.

"What are you standing in the door for?" she said. "Take off your overcoats and come into the salon."

The medico and the painter went into the salon, still speaking Italian. Vassiliev followed them irresolutely.

"Gentlemen, take off your overcoats," said the lackey stiffly. "You're not allowed in as you are."

Besides the fair girl there was another woman in the salon, very stout and tall, with a foreign face and bare arms. She sat by the piano, with a game of patience spread on her knees. She took no notice of the guests.

"Where are the other girls?" asked the medico.

"They're drinking tea," said the fair one. "Stiepan," she called out. "Go and tell the girls some students have come!"

A little later a third girl entered, in a bright red dress with blue stripes. Her face was thickly and unskilfully painted. Her forehead was hidden under her hair. She stared with dull, frightened eyes. As she came she immediately began to sing in a strong hoarse contralto. After her a fourth girl. After her a fifth.

In all this Vassiliev saw nothing new or curious. It seemed to him that he had seen before, and more than once, this salon, piano, cheap gilt mirror, the white bow, the dress with blue stripes and the stupid, indifferent faces. But of darkness, quiet, mystery, and guilty smile—of all he had expected to meet here and which frightened him—he did not see even a shadow.

Everything was commonplace, prosaic, and dull. Only one thing provoked his curiosity a little, that was the terrible, as it were intentional lack of taste, which was seen in the overmantels, the absurd pictures, the dresses and the White bow. In this lack of taste there was something characteristic and singular.

"How poor and foolish it all is!" thought Vassiliev. "What is there in all this rubbish to tempt a normal man, to provoke him into committing a frightful sin, to buy a living soul for a rouble? I can understand anyone sinning for the sake of splendour, beauty, grace, passion; but what is there here? What tempts people here? But ... it's no good thinking!"

"Whiskers, stand me champagne." The fair one turned to him.

Vassiliev suddenly blushed.

"With pleasure," he said, bowing politely. "But excuse me if I ... I don't drink with you, I don't drink."

Five minutes after the friends were off to another house.

"Why did you order drinks?" stormed the medico. "What a millionaire, flinging six roubles into the gutter like that for nothing at all."

"Why shouldn't I give her pleasure if she wants it?" said Vassiliev, justifying himself.

"You didn't give her any pleasure. Madame got that. It's Madame who tells them to ask the guests for drinks. She makes by it."

"Behold the mill," the painter began to sing, "Now fall'n to ruin...."

When they came to another house the friends stood outside in the vestibule, but did not enter the salon. As in the first house, a figure rose up from the sofa in the hall, in a black jacket, with a sleepy lackey's face. As he looked at this lackey, at his face and shabby jacket, Vassiliev thought: "What must an ordinary simple Russian go through before Fate casts him up here? Where was he before, and what was he doing? What awaits him? Is he married, where's his mother, and does she know he's a lackey here?" Thenceforward in every house Vassiliev involuntarily turned his attention to the lackey first of all.

In one of the houses, it seemed to be the fourth, the lackey was a dry little, puny fellow, with a chain across his waistcoat. He was reading a newspaper and took no notice of the guests at all. Glancing at his face, Vassiliev had the idea that a fellow with a face like that could steal and murder and perjure. And indeed the face was interesting: a big forehead, grey eyes, a flat little nose, small close-set teeth, and the expression on his face dull and impudent at once, like a puppy hard on a hare. Vassiliev had the thought that he would like to touch this lackey's hair: is it rough or soft f It must be rough like a dog's.

III

Because he had had two glasses the painter suddenly got rather drunk, and unnaturally lively.

"Let's go to another place," he added, waving his hands. "I'll introduce you to the best!"

When he had taken his friends into the house which was according to him the best, he proclaimed a persistent desire to dance a quadrille. The medico began to grumble that they would have to pay the musicians a rouble but agreed to be his vis-à-vis. The dance began.

It was just as bad in the best house as in the worst. Just the same mirrors and pictures were here, the same coiffures and dresses. Looking round at the furniture and the costumes Vassiliev now understood that it was not lack of taste, but something that might be called the particular taste and style of S——v Street, quite impossible to find anywhere else, something complete, not accidental, evolved in time. After he had been to eight houses he no longer wondered at the colour of the dresses or the long trains, or at the bright bows, or the sailor dresses, or the thick violent painting of the cheeks; he understood that all this was in harmony, that if only one woman dressed herself humanly, or one decent print hung on the wall, then the general tone of the whole street would suffer.

How badly they manage the business? Can't they really understand that vice is only fascinating when it is beautiful and secret, hidden under the cloak of virtue? Modest black dresses, pale faces, sad smiles, and darkness act more strongly than this clumsy tinsel. Idiots! If they don't understand it themselves, their guests ought to teach them....

A girl in a Polish costume trimmed with white fur came up close to him and sat down by his side.

"Why don't you dance, my brown-haired darling?" she asked. "What do you fed so bored about?"

"Because it is boring."

"Stand me a Château Lafitte, then you won't be bored."

Vassiliev made no answer. For a little while he was silent, then he asked:

"What time do you go to bed as a rule?"

"Six."

"When do you get up?"

"Sometimes two, sometimes three."

"And after you get up what do you do?"

"We drink coffee. We have dinner at seven."

"And what do you have for dinner?"

"Soup or schi as a rule, beef-steak, dessert. Our madame keeps the girls well. But what are you asking all this for?"

"Just to have a talk...."

Vassiliev wanted to ask about all sorts of things. He had a strong desire to find out where she came from, were her parents alive, and did they know she was here; how she got into the house; was she happy and contented, or gloomy and depressed with dark thoughts. Does she ever hope to escape.... But he could not possibly think how to begin, or how to put his questions without seeming indiscreet. He thought for a long while and asked:

"How old are you?"

"Eighty," joked the girl, looking and laughing at the tricks the painter was doing with his hands and feet.

She suddenly giggled and uttered a long filthy expression aloud so that every one could hear.

Vassiliev, terrified, not knowing how to look, began to laugh uneasily. He alone smiled: all the others, his friends, the musicians and the women—paid no attention to his neighbour. They might never have heard.

"Stand me a Lafitte," said the girl again.

Vassiliev was suddenly repelled by her white trimming and her voice and left her. It seemed to him close and hot. His heart began to beat slowly and violently, like a hammer, one, two, three.

"Let's get out of here," he said, pulling the painter's sleeve.

"Wait. Let's finish it."

While the medico and the painter were finishing their quadrille, Vassiliev, in order to avoid the women, eyed the musicians. The pianist was a nice old man with spectacles, with a face like Marshal Basin; the fiddler a young man with a short, fair beard dressed in the latest fashion. The young man was not stupid or starved, on the contrary he looked clever, young and fresh. He was dressed with a touch of originality, and played with emotion. Problem: how did he and the decent old man get here? Why aren't they ashamed to sit here? What do they think about when they look at the women?

If the piano and the fiddle were played by ragged, hungry, gloomy, drunken creatures, with thin stupid faces, then their presence would perhaps be intelligible. As it was, Vassiliev could understand. nothing. Into his memory came the story that he had read about the unfortunate woman, and now he found that the human figure with the guilty smile had nothing to do with this. It seemed to him that they were not unfortunate women that he saw, but they belonged to another, utterly different world, foreign and inconceivable to him; if he had seen this world on the stage or read about it in a book he would never have believed it.... The girl with the white trimming giggled again and said something disgusting aloud. He felt sick, blushed, and went out:

"Wait. We're coming too," cried the painter.

IV

"I had a talk with my mam'selle while we were dancing," said the medico when all three came into the street. "The subject was her first love. He was a bookkeeper in Smolensk with a wife and five children. She was seventeen and lived with her pa and ma who kept a soap and candle shop."

"How did he conquer her heart?" asked Vassiliev.

"He bought her fifty roubles'-worth of underclothes—Lord knows what!"

"However could he get her love-story out of his girl?" thought Vassiliev. "I can't. My dear chaps, I'm off home," he said.

"Why?"

"Because I don't know how to get on here. I'm bored and disgusted. What is there amusing about it? If they were only human beings; but they're savages and beasts. I'm going, please."

"Grisha darling, please," the painter said with a sob in his voice, pressing close to Vassiliev, "let's go to one more—then to Hell with them. Do come, Grigor."

They prevailed on Vassiliev and led him up a staircase. The carpet and the gilded balustrade, the porter who opened the door, the panels which decorated the hall, were still in the same S——v Street style, but here it was perfected and imposing.

"Really I'm going home," said Vassiliev, taking off his overcoat.

"Darling, please, please," said the painter and kissed him on the neck. "Don't be so faddy, Grigri—be a pal. Together we came, together we go. What a beast you are though!"

"I can wait for you in the street. My God, it's disgusting here."

"Please, please.... You just look on, see, just look on."

"One should look at things objectively," said the medico seriously.

Vassiliev entered the salon and sat down. There were many more guests besides him and his friends: two infantry officers, a grey, bald-headed gentleman with gold spectacles, two young clean-shaven men from the Surveyors' Institute, and a very drunk man with an actor's face. All the girls were looking after these guests and took no notice of Vassiliev. Only one of them dressed like Aïda glanced at him sideways, smiled at something and said with a yawn:

"So the dark one's come."

Vassiliev's heart was beating and his face was burning. He felt ashamed for being there, disgusted and tormented. He was tortured by the thought that he, a decent and affectionate man (so he considered himself up till now), despised these women and felt nothing towards them but repulsion. He could not feel pity for them or for the musicians or the lackeys.

"It's because I don't try to understand them," he thought. "They're all more like beasts than human beings; but all the same they are human beings. They've got souls. One should understand them first, then judge them."

"Grisha, don't go away. Wait for us," called the painter; and he disappeared somewhere.

Soon the medico disappeared also.

"Yes, one should try to understand. It's no good, otherwise," thought Vassiliev, and he began to examine intently the face of each girl, looking for the guilty smile. But whether he could not read faces or because none of these women felt guilty he saw in each face only a dull look of common, vulgar boredom and satiety. Stupid eyes, stupid smiles, harsh, stupid voices, impudent gestures—and nothing else. Evidently every woman had in her past a love romance with a bookkeeper and fifty roubles'-worth of underclothes. And in the present the only good things in life were coffee, a three-course dinner, wine, quadrilles, and sleeping till two in the afternoon....

Finding not one guilty smile, Vassiliev began to examine them to see if even one looked clever and his attention was arrested by one pale, rather tired face. It was that of a dark woman no longer young, wearing a dress scattered with spangles. She sat in a chair staring at the floor and thinking of something. Vassiliev paced up and down and then sat down beside her as if by accident.

"One must begin with something trivial," he thought, "and gradually pass on to serious conversation...."

"What a beautiful little dress you have on," he said, and touched the gold fringe of her scarf with his finger.

"It's all right," said the dark woman.

"Where do you come from?"

"I? A long way. From Tchernigov."

"It's a nice part."

"It always is, where you don't happen to be."

"What a pity I can't describe nature," thought Vassiliev. "I'd move her by descriptions of Tchernigov. She must love it if she was born there."

"Do you feel lonely here?" he asked.

"Of course I'm lonely."

"Why don't you go away from here, if you're lonely?"

"Where shall I go to? Start begging, eh?"

"It's easier to beg than to live here."

"Where did you get that idea? Have you been a beggar?"

"I begged, when I hadn't enough to pay my university fees; and even if I hadn't begged it's easy enough to understand. A beggar is a free man, at any rate, and you're a slave."

The dark woman stretched herself, and followed with sleepy eyes the lackey who carried a tray of glasses and soda-water.

"Stand us a champagne," she said, and yawned again.

"Champagne," said Vassiliev. "What would happen if your mother or your brother suddenly came in? What would you say? And what would they say? You would say 'champagne' then."

Suddenly the noise of crying was heard. From the next room where the lackey had carried the soda-water, a fair man rushed out with a red face and angry eyes. He was followed by the tall, stout madame, who screamed in a squeaky voice:

"No one gave you permission to slap the girls in the face. Better class than you come here, and never slap a girl. You bounder!"

Followed an uproar. Vassiliev was scared and went white. In the next room some one wept, sobbing, sincerely, as only the insulted weep. And he understood that indeed human beings lived here, actually human beings, who get offended, suffer, weep, and ask for help. The smouldering hatred, the feeling of repulsion, gave way to an acute sense of pity and anger against the wrong-doer. He rushed into the room from which the weeping came. Through the rows of bottles which stood on the marble table-top he saw a suffering tear-stained face, stretched out his hands towards this face, stepped to the table and instantly gave a leap back in terror. The sobbing woman was dead-drunk.

As he made his way through the noisy crowd, gathered round the fair man, his heart failed him, he lost his courage like a boy, and it seemed to him that in this foreign, inconceivable world, they wanted to run after him, to beat him, to abuse him with foul words. He tore down his coat from the peg and rushed headlong down the stairs.

V

Pressing dose to the fence, he stood near to the house and waited for his friends to come out. The sounds of the pianos and fiddles, gay, bold, impudent and sad, mingled into chaos in the air, and this confusion was, as before, as if an unseen orchestra were tuning in the dark over the roof-tops. If he looked up towards the darkness, then all the background was scattered with white, moving points: it was snowing. The flakes, coming into the light, spun lazily in the air like feathers, and still more lazily fell. Flakes of snow crowded whirling about Vassiliev, and hung on his beard, his eyelashes, his eyebrows. The cabmen, the horses, and the passers-by, all were white.

"How dare the snow fall in this street?" thought Vassiliev. "A curse on these houses."

Because of his headlong rush down the staircase his feet failed him from weariness; he was out of breath as if he had climbed a mountain. His heart beat so loud that he could hear it. A longing came over him to get out of this street as soon as possible and go home; but still stronger was his desire to wait for his friends and to vent upon them his feeling of heaviness.

He had not understood many things in the houses. The souls of the perishing women were to him a mystery as before; but it was dear to him that the business was much worse than one would have thought. If the guilty woman who poisoned herself was called a prostitute, then it was hard to find a suitable name for all these creatures, who danced to the muddling music and said long, disgusting phrases. They were not perishing; they were already done for.

"Vice is here," he thought; "but there is neither confession of sin nor hope of salvation. They are bought and sold, drowned in wine and torpor, and they are dull and indifferent as sheep and do not understand. My God, my God!"

It was so dear to him that all that which is called human dignity, individuality, the image and likeness of God, was here dragged down to the gutter, as they say of drunkards, and that not only the street and the stupid women were to blame for it.

A crowd of students white with snow, talking and laughing gaily, passed by. One of them, a tall, thin man, peered into Vassiliev's face and said drunkenly, "He's one of ours. Logged, old man? Aha! my lad. Never mind. Walk up, never say die, uncle."

He took Vassiliev by the shoulders and pressed his cold wet moustaches to his cheek, then slipped, staggered, brandished his arms, and cried out:

"Steady there—don't fall."

Laughing, he ran to join his comrades.

Through the noise the painter's voice became audible.

"You dare beat women! I won't have it. Go to Hell. You're regular swine."

The medico appeared at the door of the house. He glanced round and on seeing Vassiliev, said in alarm:

"Is that you? My God, it's simply impossible to go anywhere with Yegor. I can't understand a chap like that. He kicked up a row—can't you hear? Yegor," he called from the door. "Yegor!"

"I won't have you hitting women." The painter's shrill voice was audible again from upstairs.

Something heavy and bulky tumbled down the staircase. It was the painter coming head over heels. He had evidently been thrown out.

He lifted himself up from the ground, dusted his hat, and with an angry indignant face, shook his fist at the upstairs.

"Scoundrels! Butchers! Bloodsuckers! I won't have you hitting a weak, drunken woman. Ah, you...."

"Yegor ... Yegor!" the medico began to implore, "I give my word I'll never go out with you again. Upon my honour, I won't."

The painter gradually calmed, and the friends went home.

"To these sad shores unknowing"—the medico began—"An unknown power entices...."

"Behold the mill," the painter sang with him after a pause, "Now fallen into ruin." How the snow is falling, most Holy Mother. Why did you go away, Grisha? You're a coward; you're only an old woman."

Vassiliev was walking behind his friends. He stared at their backs and thought: "One of two things: either prostitution only seems to us an evil and we exaggerate it, or if prostitution is really such an evil as is commonly thought, these charming friends of mine are just as much slavers, violators, and murderers as the inhabitants of Syria and Cairo whose photographs appear in 'The Field.' They're singing, laughing, arguing soundly now, but haven't they just been exploiting starvation, ignorance, and stupidity? They have, I saw them at it. Where does their humanity, their science, and their painting come in, then? The science, art, and lofty sentiments of these murderers remind me of the lump of fat in the story. Two robbers killed a beggar in a forest; they began to divide his clothes between themselves and found in his bag a lump of pork fat. 'In the nick of time,' said one of them. 'Let's have a bite!' 'How can you?' the other cried in terror. 'Have you forgotten today's Friday?' So they refrained from eating. After having cut the man's throat they walked out of the forest confident that they were pious fellows. These two are just the same. When they've paid for women they go and imagine they're painters and scholars....

"Listen, you two," he said angrily and sharply. "Why do you go to those places? Can't you understand how horrible they are? Your medicine tells you every one of these women dies prematurely from consumption or something else; your arts tell you that she died morally still earlier. Each of them dies because during her lifetime she accepts on an average, let us say, five hundred men. Each of them is killed by five hundred men, and you're amongst the five hundred. Now if each of you comes here and to places like this two hundred and fifty times in his lifetime, then it means that between you you have killed one woman. Can't you understand that? Isn't it horrible?"

"Ah, isn't this awful, my God?"

"There, I knew it would end like this," said the painter frowning. "We oughtn't to have had anything to do with this fool of a blockhead. I suppose you think your head's full of great thoughts and great ideas now. Devil knows what they are, but they're not ideas. You're staring at me now with hatred and disgust; but if you want my opinion you'd better build twenty more of the houses than look like that. There's more vice in your look than in the whole street. Let's dear out, Volodya, damn him! He's a fool. He's a blockhead, and that's all he is."

"Human beings are always killing each other," said the medico. "That is immoral, of course. But philosophy won't help you. Good-bye!"

The friends parted at Trubnoi Square and went their way. Left alone, Vassiliev began to stride along the boulevard. He was frightened of the dark, frightened of the snow, which fell to the earth in little flakes, but seemed to long to cover the whole world; he was frightened of the street-lamps, which glimmered faintly through the clouds of snow. An inexplicable faint-hearted fear possessed his soul. Now and then people passed him; but he gave a start and stepped aside. It seemed to him that from everywhere there came and stared at him women, only women....

"It's coming on," he thought, "I'm going to have a fit."

VI

At home he lay on his bed and began to talk, shivering all over his body.

"Live women, live.... My God, they're alive."

He sharpened the edge of his imagination in every possible way. Now he was the brother of an unfortunate, now her father. Now he was himself a fallen woman, with painted cheeks; and all this terrified him.

It seemed to him somehow that he must solve this question immediately, at all costs, and that the problem was not strange to him, but was his own. He made a great effort, conquered his despair, and, sitting on the side of the bed, his head clutched in his hands, he began to think:

How could all the women he had seen that night be saved? The process of solving a problem was familiar to him as to a learned person; and notwithstanding all his excitement he kept strictly to this process. He recalled to mind the history of the question, its literature, and just after three o'clock he was pacing up and down, trying to remember all the experiments which are practised nowadays for the salvation of women. He had a great many good friends who lived in furnished rooms, Falzfein, Galyashkin, Nechaiev, Yechkin ... not a few among them were honest and self-sacrificing, and some of them had attempted to save these women....

All these few attempts, thought Vassiliev, rare attempts, may be divided into three groups. Some having rescued a woman from a brothel hired a room for her, bought her a sewing-machine and she became a dressmaker, and the man who saved her kept her for his mistress, openly or otherwise, but later when he had finished his studies and was going away, he would hand her over to another decent fellow. So the fallen woman remained fallen. Others after having bought her out also hired a room for her, bought the inevitable sewing-machine and started her off reading and writing and preached at her. The woman sits and sews as long as it is novel and amusing, but later, when she is bored, she begins to receive men secretly, or runs back to where she can sleep till three in the afternoon, drink coffee, and eat till she is full. Finally, the most ardent and self-sacrificing take a bold, determined step. They marry, and when the impudent, self-indulgent, stupefied creature becomes a wife, a lady of the house, and then a mother, her life and outlook are utterly changed, and in the wife and mother it is hard to recognise the unfortunate woman. Yes, marriage is the best, it may be the only, resource.

"But it's impossible," Vassiliev said aloud and threw himself down on his bed. "First of all, I could not marry one. One would have to be a saint to be able to do it, unable to hate, not knowing disgust. But let us suppose that the painter, the medico, and I got the better of our feelings and married, that all these women got married, what is the result? What kind of effect follows? The result is that while the women get married here in Moscow, the Smolensk bookkeeper seduces a fresh lot, and these will pour into the empty places, together with women from Saratov, Nijni-Novgorod, Warsaw.... And what happens to the hundred thousand in London? What can be done with those in Hamburg?

The oil in the lamp was used up and the lamp began to smell. Vassiliev did not notice it. Again he began to pace up and down, thinking. Now he put the question differently. What can be done to remove the demand for fallen women? For this it is necessary that the men who buy and kill them should at once begin to feel all the immorality of their rôle of slave-owners, and this should terrify them. It is necessary to save the men.

Science and art apparently won't do, thought Vassiliev. There is only one way out—to be an apostle.

And he began to dream how he would stand to-morrow evening at the corner of the street and say to each passer-by: "Where are you going and what for? Fear God!"

He would turn to the indifferent cabmen and say to them:

"Why are you standing here? Why don't you revolt? You do believe in God, don't you? And you do know that this is a crime, and that people will go to Hell for this? Why do you keep quiet, then? True, the women are strangers to you, but they have fathers and brothers exactly the same as you...."

Some friend of Vassiliev's once said of him that he was a man of talent. There is a talent for writing, for the theatre, for painting; but Vassiliev's was peculiar, a talent for humanity. He had a fine and noble flair for every kind of suffering. As a good actor reflects in himself the movement and voice of another, so Vassiliev could reflect in himself another's pain. Seeing tears, he wept. With a sick person, he himself became sick and moaned. If he saw violence done, it seemed to him that he was the victim. He was frightened like a child, and, frightened, ran for help. Another's pain roused him, excited him, threw him into a state of ecstasy....

Whether the friend was right I do not know, but what happened to Vassiliev when it seemed to him that the question was solved was very much like an ecstasy. He sobbed, laughed, said aloud the things he would say to-morrow, felt a burning love for the men who would listen to him and stand by his side at the corner of the street, preaching. He sat down to write to them; he made vows.

All this was the more like an ecstasy in that it did not last. Vassiliev was soon tired. The London women, the Hamburg women, those from Warsaw, crushed him with their mass, as the mountains crush the earth. He quailed before this mass; he lost himself; he remembered he had no gift for speaking, that he was timid and faint-hearted, that strange people would hardly want to listen to and understand him, a law-student in his third year, a frightened and insignificant figure. The true apostleship consisted, not only in preaching, but also in deeds....

When daylight came and the carts rattled on the streets, Vassiliev lay motionless on the sofa, staring at one point. He did not think any more of women, or men, or apostles. All his attention was fixed on the pain of his soul which tormented him. It was a dull pain, indefinite, vague; it was like anguish and the most acute fear and despair. He could say where the pain was. It was in his breast, under the heart. It could not be compared to anything. Once on a time he used to have violent toothache. Once, he had pleurisy and neuralgia. But all these pains were as nothing beside the pain of his soul. Beneath this pain life seemed repulsive. The thesis, his brilliant work already written, the people he loved, the salvation of fallen women, all that which only yesterday he loved or was indifferent to, remembered now, irritated him in the same way as the noise of the carts, the running about of the porters and the daylight.... If someone now were to perform before his eyes a deed of mercy or an act of revolting violence, both would produce upon him an equally repulsive impression. Of all the thoughts which roved lazily in his head, two only did not irritate him: one—at any moment he had the power to kill himself, the other—that the pain would not last more than three days. The second he knew from experience.

After having lain down for a while he got up and walked wringing his hands, not from corner to corner as usually, but in a square along the walls. He caught a glimpse of himself in the glass. His face was pale and haggard, his temples hollow, his eyes bigger, darker, more immobile, as if they were not his own, and they expressed the intolerable suffering of his soul.

In the afternoon the painter knocked at the door.

"Gregory, are you at home?" he asked.

Receiving no answer, he stood musing for a while, and said to himself good-naturedly:

"Out. He's gone to the University. Damn him."

And went away.

Vassiliev lay down on his bed and burying his head in the pillow he began to cry with the pain. But the faster his tears flowed, the more terrible was the pain. When it was dark, he got into his mind the idea of the horrible night which was awaiting him and awful despair seized him. He dressed quickly, ran out of his room, leaving the door wide open, and into the street without reason or purpose. Without asking himself where he was going, he walked quickly to Sadovaia Street.

Snow was falling as yesterday. It was thawing. Putting his hands into his sleeves, shivering, and frightened of the noises and the bells of the trams and of passers-by, Vassiliev walked from Sadovaia to Sukhariev Tower then to the Red Gates, and from here he turned and went to Basmannaia. He went into a public-house and gulped down a big glass of vodka, but felt no better. Arriving at Razgoulyai, he turned to the right and began to stride down streets that he had never in his life been down before. He came to that old bridge under which the river Yaouza roars and from whence long rows of lights are seen in the windows of the Red Barracks. In order to distract the pain of his soul by a new sensation or another pain, not knowing what to do, weeping and trembling, Vassiliev unbuttoned his coat and jacket, baring his naked breast to the damp snow and the wind. Neither lessened the pain. Then he bent over the rail of the bridge and stared down at the black, turbulent Yaouza, and he suddenly wanted to throw himself head-first, not from hatred of life, not for the sake of suicide, but only to hurt himself and so to kill one pain by another. But the black water, the dark, deserted banks covered with snow were frightening. He shuddered and went on. He walked as far as the Red Barracks, then back and into a wood, from the wood to the bridge again.

"No! Home, home," he thought. "At home I believe it's easier."

And he went back. On returning home he tore off his wet clothes and hat, began to pace along the walls, and paced incessantly until the very morning.

VII

The next morning when the painter and the medico came to see him, they found him in a shirt torn to ribbons, his hands bitten all over, tossing about in the room and moaning with pain.

"For God's sake!" he began to sob, seeing his comrades, "Take me anywhere you like, do what you like, but save me, for God's sake now, now! I'll kill myself."

The painter went pale and was bewildered. The medico, too, nearly began to cry; but, believing that medical men must be cool and serious on every occasion of life, he said coldly:

"It's a fit you've got. But never mind. Come to the doctor, at once."

"Anywhere you like, but quickly, for God's sake!"

"Don't be agitated. You must struggle with yourself."

The painter and the medico dressed Vassiliev with trembling hands and led him into the street.

"Mikhail Sergueyich has been wanting to make your acquaintance for a long while," the medico said on the way. "He's a very nice man, and knows his job splendidly. He took his degree in '82, and has got a huge practice already. He keeps friends with the students."

"Quicker, quicker...." urged Vassiliev. Mikhail Sergueyich, a stout doctor with fair hair, received the friends politely, firmly, coldly, and smiled with one cheek only.

"The painter and Mayer have told me of your disease already," he said. "Very glad to be of service to you. Well? Sit down, please."

He made Vassiliev sit down in a big chair by the table, and put a box of cigarettes in front of him.

"Well?" he began, stroking his knees. "Let's make a start. How old are you?"

He put questions and the medico answered. He asked whether Vassiliev's father suffered from any peculiar diseases, if he had fits of drinking, was he distinguished by his severity or any other eccentricities. He asked the same questions about his grandfather, mother, sisters, and brothers. Having ascertained that his mother had a fine voice and occasionally appeared on the stage, he suddenly brightened up and asked:

"Excuse me, but could you recall whether the theatre was not a passion with your mother?"

About twenty minutes passed. Vassiliev was bored by the doctor stroking his knees and talking of the same thing all the while.

"As far as I can understand your questions, Doctor," he said. "You want to know whether my disease is hereditary or not. It is not hereditary."

The doctor went on to ask if Vassiliev had not any secret vices in his early youth, any blows on the head, any love passions, eccentricities, or exceptional infatuations. To half the questions habitually asked by careful doctors you may return no answer without any injury to your health; but Mikhail Sergueyich, the medico and the painter looked as though, if Vassiliev failed to answer even one single question, everything would be ruined. For some reason the doctor wrote down the answers he received on a scrap of paper. Discovering that Vassiliev had already passed through the faculty of natural science and was now in the Law faculty, the doctor began to be pensive....

"He wrote a brilliant thesis last year...." said the medico.

"Excuse me. You mustn't interrupt me; you prevent me from concentrating," the doctor said, smiling with one cheek. "Yes, certainly that is important for the anamnesis.... Yes, yes.... And do you drink vodka?" he turned to Vassiliev.

"Very rarely."

Another twenty minutes passed. The medico began sotto voce to give his opinion of the immediate causes of the fit and told how he, the painter and Vassiliev went to S——v Street the day before yesterday.

The indifferent, reserved, cold tone in which his friends and the doctor were speaking of the women and the miserable street seemed to him in the highest degree strange....

"Doctor, tell me this one thing," he said, restraining himself from being rude. "Is prostitution an evil or not?"

"My dear fellow, who disputes it?" the doctor said with an expression as though he had long ago solved all these questions for himself. "Who disputes it?"

"Are you a psychiatrist?"

"Yes-s, a psychiatrist."

"Perhaps all of you are right," said Vassiliev, rising and beginning to walk from corner to corner. "It may be. But to me all this seems amazing. They see a great achievement in my having passed through two faculties at the university; they praise me to the skies because I have written a work that will be thrown away and forgotten in three years' time, but became I can't speak of prostitutes as indifferently as I can about these chairs, they send me to doctors, call me a lunatic, and pity me."

For some reason Vassiliev suddenly began to feel an intolerable pity for himself, his friends, and everybody whom he had seen the day before yesterday, and for the doctor. He began to sob and fell into the chair.

The friends looked interrogatively at the doctor. He, looking as though he magnificently understood the tears and the despair, and knew himself a specialist in this line, approached Vassiliev and gave him some drops to drink, and then when Vassiliev grew calm undressed him and began to examine the sensitiveness of his skin, of the knee reflexes....

And Vassiliev felt better. When he was coming out of the doctor's he was already ashamed; the noise of the traffic did not seem irritating, and the heaviness beneath his heart became easier and easier as though it were thawing. In his hand were two prescriptions. One was for kali-bromatum, the other—morphia. He used to take both before.

He stood still in the street for a while, pensive, and then, taking leave of his friends, lazily dragged on towards the university.

MISFORTUNE

Sophia Pietrovna, the wife of the solicitor Loubianzev, a handsome young woman of about twenty-five, was walking quickly along a forest path with her bungalow neighbour, the barrister Ilyin. It was just after four. In the distance, above the path, white feathery clouds gathered; from behind them some bright blue pieces of cloud showed through. The clouds were motionless, as if caught on the tops of the tall, aged fir trees. It was calm and warm.

In the distance the path was cut across by a low railway embankment, along which at this hour, for some reason or other, a sentry strode. Just behind the embankment a big, six-towered church with a rusty roof shone white.

"I did not expect to meet you here," Sophia Pietrovna was saying, looking down and touching the last year's leaves with the end of her parasol. "But now I am glad to have met you. I want to speak to you seriously and finally. Ivan Mikhailovich, if you really love and respect me I implore you to stop pursuing me i You follow me like a shadow—there's such a wicked look in your eye—you make love to me—write extraordinary letters and ... I don't know how all this is going to end—Good Heavens! What can all this lead to?"

Ilyin was silent. Sophia Pietrovna took a few steps and continued:

"And this sudden complete change has happened in two or three weeks after five years of friendship. I do not know you any more, Ivan Mikhailovich."

Sophia Pietrovna glanced sideways at her companion. He was staring intently, screwing up his eyes at the feathery clouds. The expression of his face was angry, capricious and distracted, like that of a man who suffers and at the same time must listen to nonsense.

"It is annoying that you yourself can't realise it!" Madame Loubianzev continued, shrugging her shoulders. "Please understand that you're not playing a very nice game. I am married, I love and respect my husband.

I have a daughter. Don't you really care in the slightest for all this? Besides, as an old friend, you know my views on family life ... on the sanctity of the home, generally."

Ilyin gave an angry grunt and sighed:

"The sanctity of the home," he murmured, "Good Lord!"

"Yes, yes. I love and respect my husband and at any rate the peace of my family life is precious to me. I'd sooner let myself be killed than be the cause of Andrey's or his daughter's unhappiness. So, please, Ivan Mikhailovich, for goodness' sake, leave me alone. Let us be good and dear friends, and give up these sighings and gaspings which don't suit you. It's settled and done with! Not another word about it. Let us talk of something else!"

Sophia Pietrovna again glanced sideways at Ilyin. He was looking up. He was pale, and angrily he bit his trembling lips. Madame Loubianzev could not understand why he was disturbed and angry, but his pallor moved her.

"Don't be cross. Let's be friends," she said, sweetly.

"Agreed! Here is my hand."

Ilyin took her tiny plump hand in both his, pressed it and slowly raised it to his lips.

"I'm not a schoolboy," he murmured. "I'm not in the least attracted by the idea of friendship with the woman I love."

"That's enough. Stop! It is all settled and done with. We have come as far as the bench. Let us sit down...."

A sweet sense of repose filled Sophia Pietrovna's soul. The most difficult and delicate thing was already said. The tormenting question was settled and done with. Now she could breathe easily and look straight at Ilyin. She looked at him, and the egotistical sense of superiority that a woman feels over her lover caressed her pleasantly. She liked the way this big strong man with a virile angry face and a huge black beard sat obediently at her side and hung his head. They were silent for a little while. "Nothing is yet settled and done with," Ilyin began. "You are reading me a sermon. 'I love and respect my husband ... the sanctity of the home....' I know all that for myself and I can tell you more. Honestly and sincerely I confess that I consider my conduct as criminal and immoral. What else? But why say what is known already? Instead of sermonizing you had far better tell me what I am to do."

"I have already told you. Go away."

"I have gone. You know quite well. I have started five times and half-way there I have come back again. I can show you the through tickets. I have kept them all safe. But I haven't the power to run away from you. I struggle frightfully, but what in Heaven's name is the use? If I cannot harden myself, if I'm weak and faint-hearted. I can't fight nature. Do you understand? I cannot! I run away from her and she holds me back by my coattails. Vile, vulgar weakness."

Ilyin blushed, got up, and began walking by the bench:

"How I hate and despise myself. Good Lord, I'm like a vicious boy—running after another man's wife, writing idiotic letters, degrading myself. Ach!" He clutched his head, grunted and sit down.

"And now comes your lack of sincerity into the bargain," he continued with bitterness. "If you don't think I am playing a nice game—why are you here? What drew you? In my letters I only ask you for a straightforward answer: Yes, or No; and instead of giving it me, every day you contrive that we shall meet 'by chance' and you treat me to quotations from a moral copy-book."

Madame Loubianzev reddened and got frightened. She suddenly felt the kind of awkwardness that a modest woman would feel at being suddenly discovered naked.

"You seem to suspect some deceit on my side," she murmured. "I have always given you a straight answer; and I asked you for one to-day."

"Ah, does one ask such things? If you had said to me at once 'Go away,' I would have gone long ago, but you never told me to. Never once have you been frank. Strange irresolution. My God, either you're playing with me, or...."

Ilyin did not finish, and rested his head in his hands. Sophia Pietrovna recalled her behaviour all through. She remembered that she had felt all these days not only in deed but even in her most intimate thoughts opposed to Ilyin's love. But at the same moment she knew that there was a grain of truth in the barrister's words. And not knowing what kind of truth it was she could not think, no matter how much she thought about it, what to say to him in answer to his complaint. It was awkward being silent, so she said shrugging her shoulders:

"So I'm to blame for that too?"

"I don't blame you for your insincerity," sighed Ilyin. "It slipped out unconsciously. Your insincerity is natural to you, in the natural order of things as well. If all mankind were to agree suddenly to become serious, everything would go to the Devil, to ruin."

Sophia Pietrovna was not in the mood for philosophy; but she was glad of the opportunity to change the conversation and asked:

"Why indeed?"

"Because only savages and animals are sincere. Since civilisation introduced into society the demand, for instance, for such a luxury as woman's virtue, sincerity has been out of place."

Angrily Ilyin began to thrust his stick into the sand. Madame Loubianzev listened without understanding much of it; she liked the conversation. First of all, she was pleased that a gifted man should speak to her, an average woman, about intellectual things; also it gave her great pleasure to watch how the pale, lively, still angry, young face was working. Much she did not understand; but the fine courage of modern man was revealed to her, the courage by which he without reflection or surmise solves the great questions and constructs his simple conclusions.

Suddenly she discovered that she was admiring him, and it frightened her.

"Pardon, but I don't really understand," she hastened to say. "Why did you mention insincerity? I entreat you once more, be a dear, good friend and leave me alone. Sincerely, I ask it."

"Good—I'll do my best. But hardly anything will come of it. Either I'll put a bullet through my brains or ... I'll start drinking in the stupidest possible way. Things will end badly for me. Everything has its limit, even a struggle with nature. Tell me now, how can one struggle with madness? If you've drunk wine, how can you get over the excitement? What can I do if your image has grown into my soul, and stands incessantly before my eyes, night and day, as plain as that fir tree there? Tell me then what thing I must do to get out of this wretched, unhappy state, when all my thoughts, desires, and dreams belong, not to me, but to some devil that has got hold of me? I love you, I love you so much that I've turned away from my path, given up my career and my closest friends, forgot my God. Never in my life have I loved so much."

Sophia Pietrovna, who was not expecting this turn, drew her body away from Ilyin, and glanced at him frightened. Tears shone in his eyes. His lips trembled, and a hungry, suppliant expression showed over all his face.

"I love you," he murmured, bringing his own eyes near to her big, frightened ones. "You are so beautiful. I'm suffering now; but I swear I could remain so all my life, suffering and looking into your eyes, but.... Keep silent, I implore you."

Sophia Pietrovna as if taken unawares began, quickly, quickly, to think out words with which to stop him. "I shall go away," she decided, but no sooner had she moved to get up, than Ilyin was on his knees at her feet already. He embraced her knees, looked into her eyes and spoke passionately, ardently, beautifully. She did not hear his words, for her fear and agitation. Somehow now at this dangerous moment when her knees pleasantly contracted, as in a warm bath, she sought with evil intention to read some meaning into her sensation. She was angry because the whole of her instead of protesting virtue was filled with weakness, laziness, and emptiness, like a drunken man to whom the ocean is but knee-deep; only in the depths of her soul, a little remote malignant voice teased: "Why don't you go away? Then this is right, is it?"

Seeking in herself an explanation she could not understand why she had not withdrawn the hand to which Ilyin's lips clung like a leech, nor why, at the same time as Ilyin, she looked hurriedly right and left to see that they were not observed.

The fir-trees and the clouds stood motionless, and gazed at them severely like broken-down masters who see something going on, but have been bribed not to report to the head. The sentry on the embankment stood like a stick and seemed to be staring at the bench. "Let him look!" thought Sophia Pietrovna.

"But ... But listen," she said at last with despair in her voice. "What will this lead to? What will happen afterwards?"

"I don't know. I don't know," he began to whisper, waving these unpleasant questions aside.

The hoarse, jarring whistle of a railway engine became audible. This cold, prosaic sound of the everyday world made Madame Loubianzev start.

"It's time, I must go," she said, getting up quickly. "The train is coming. Audrey is arriving. He will want his dinner."

Sophia Pietrovna turned her blazing cheeks to the embankment. First the engine came slowly into sight, after it the carriages. It was not a bungalow train, but a goods train. In a long row, one after another like the days of man's life, the cars drew past the white background of the church, and there seemed to be no end to them.

But at last the train disappeared, and the end car with the guard and the lighted lamps disappeared into the green. Sophia Pietrovna turned sharply and not looking at Ilyin began to walk quickly back along the path. She had herself in control again. Red with shame, offended, not by Ilyin, no I but by the cowardice and shamelessness with which she, a good, respectable woman allowed a stranger to embrace her knees. She had only one thought now, to reach her bungalow and her family as quickly as possible. The barrister could hardly keep up with her. Turning from the path on to a little track, she glanced at him so quickly that she noticed only the sand on his knees, and she motioned with her hand at him to let her be.

Running into the house Sophia Pietrovna stood for about five minutes motionless in her room, looking now at the window then at the writing table.... "You disgraceful woman," she scolded herself; "disgraceful!" In spite of herself she recollected every detail, hiding nothing, how all these days she had been against Ilyin's love-making, yet she was somehow drawn to meet him and explain; but besides this when he was lying at her feet she felt an extraordinary pleasure. She recalled everything, not sparing herself, and now, stifled with shame, she could have slapped her own face.

"Poor Andrey," she thought, trying, as she remembered her husband, to give her face the tenderest possible expression—"Varya, my poor darling child, does not know what a mother she has. Forgive me, my dears. I love you very much ... very much!..."

And wishing to convince herself that she was still a good wife and mother, that corruption had not yet touched those "sanctities" of hers, of which she had spoken to Ilyin, Sophia Pietrovna ran into the kitchen and scolded the cook for not having laid the table for Andrey Ilyitch. She tried to imagine her husband's tired, hungry look, and pitying him aloud, she laid the table herself, a thing which she had never done before. Then she found her daughter Varya, lifted her up in her hands and kissed her passionately; the child seemed to her heavy and cold, but she would not own it to herself, and she began to tell her what a good, dear, splendid father she had.

But when, soon after, Andrey. Ilyitch arrived, she barely greeted him. The flow of imaginary feelings had ebbed away without convincing her of anything; she was only exasperated and enraged by the lie. She sat at the window, suffered, and raged. Only in distress can people understand how difficult it is to master their thoughts and feelings. Sophia Pietrovna said afterwards a confusion was going on inside her as hard to define as to count a cloud of swiftly flying sparrows. Thus from the fact that she was delighted at her husband's arrival and pleased with the way he behaved at dinner, she suddenly concluded that she had begun to hate him. Andrey Ilyitch, languid with hunger and fatigue, while waiting for the soup, fell upon the sausage and ate it greedily, chewing loudly and moving his temples.

"My God," thought Sophia Pietrovna. "I do love and respect him, but ... why does he chew so disgustingly."

Her thoughts were no less disturbed than her feelings. Madame Loubianzev, like all who have no experience of the struggle with unpleasant thought, did her best not to think of her unhappiness, and the more zealously she tried, the more vivid Ilyin became to her imagination, the sand on his knees, the feathery clouds, the train....

"Why did I—idiot—go to-day?" she teased herself. "And am I really a person who can't answer for herself?"

Fear has big eyes. When Andrey Ilyitch had finished the last course, she had already resolved to tell him everything and so escape from danger.

"Andrey, I want to speak to you seriously," she began after dinner, when her husband was taking off his coat and boots in order to have a lie down.

"Well?"

"Let's go away from here!"

"How—where to? It's still too early to go to town."

"No. Travel or something like that."

"Travel," murmured the solicitor, stretching himself. "I dream of it myself, but where shall I get the money, and who'll look after my business."

After a little reflection he added:

"Yes, really you are bored. Go by yourself if you want to."

Sophia Pietrovna agreed; but at the same time she saw that Ilyin would be glad of the opportunity to travel in the same train with her, in the same carriage....

She pondered and looked at her husband, who was full fed but still languid. For some reason her eyes stopped on his feet, tiny, almost womanish, in stupid socks. On the toe of both socks little threads were standing out. Under the drawn blind a bumble bee was knocking against the window pane and buzzing. Sophia Pietrovna stared at the threads, listened to the bumble bee and pictured her journey.... Day and night Ilyin sits opposite, without taking his eyes from her, angry with his weakness and pale with the pain of his soul. He brands himself as a libertine, accuses her, tears his hair; but when the dark comes he seizes the chance when the passengers go to sleep or alight at a station and falls on his knees before her and clasps her feet, as he did by the bench....

She realised that she was dreaming....

"Listen. I am not going by myself," she said. "You must come, too!"

"Sophochka, that's all imagination!" sighed Loubianzev. "You must be serious and only ask for the possible...."

"You'll come when you And out!" thought Sophia Pietrovna.

Having decided to go away at all costs, she began to feel free from danger; her thoughts fell gradually into order, she became cheerful and even allowed herself to think about everything. Whatever she may think or dream about, she is going all the same. While her husband still slept, little by little, evening came....

She sat in the drawing-room playing the piano. Outside the window the evening animation, the sound of music, but chiefly the thought of her own cleverness in mastering her misery gave the final touch to her joy. Other women, her easy conscience told her, in a position like her own would surely not resist, they would spin round like a whirlwind; but she was nearly burnt up with shame, she suffered and now she had escaped from a danger which perhaps was nonexistent! Her virtue and resolution moved her so much that she even glanced at herself in the glass three times.

When it was dark visitors came. The men sat down to cards in the dining-room, the ladies were in the drawing room and on the terrace. Ilyin came last, he was stem and gloomy and looked ill. He sat down on a corner of the sofa and did not get up for the whole evening. Usually cheerful and full of conversation, he was now silent, frowning, and rubbing his eyes. When he had to answer a question he smiled with difficulty and only with his upper lip, answering abruptly and spitefully. He made about five jokes in all, but his jokes seemed crude and insolent. It seemed to Sophia Pietrovna that he was on the brink of hysteria. But only now as she sat at the piano did she acknowledge that the unhappy man was not in the mood to joke, that he was sick in his soul, he could find no place for himself. It was for her sake he was ruining the best days of his career and his youth, wasting his last farthing on a bungalow, had left his mother and sisters uncared for, and, above all, was breaking down under the martyrdom of his struggle. From simple, common humanity she ought to take him seriously....

All this was dear to her, even to paining her. If she were to go up to Ilyin now and say to him "No," there would be such strength in her voice that it would be hard to disobey. But she did not go up to him and she did not say it, did not even think it.... The petty selfishness of a young nature seemed never to have been revealed in her as strongly as that evening. She admitted that Byin was unhappy and that he sat on the sofa as if on hot coals. She was sorry for him, but at the same time the presence of the man who loved her so desperately filled her with a triumphant sense of her own power. She felt her youth, her beauty, her inaccessibility, and—since she had decided to go away—she gave herself full rein this evening. She coquetted, laughed continually, she sang with singular emotion, and as one inspired. Everything made her gay and everything seemed funny. It amused her to recall the incident of the bench, the sentry looking on. The visitors seemed funny to her, Ilyin's insolent jokes, his tie pin which she had never seen before. The pin was a little red snake with tiny diamond eyes; the snake seemed so funny that she was ready to kiss and kiss it.

Sophia Pietrovna, nervously sang romantic songs, with a kind of half-intoxication, and as if jeering at another's sorrow she chose sad, melancholy songs that spoke of lost hopes, of the past, of old age.... "And old age is approaching nearer and nearer," she sang. What had she to do with old age?

"There's something wrong going on in me," she thought now and then through laughter and singing.

At twelve o'clock the visitors departed. Ilyin was the last to go. She still felt warm enough about him to go with him to the lower step of the terrace. She had the idea of telling him that she was going away with her husband, just to see what effect this news would have upon him.

The moon was hiding behind the clouds, but it was so bright that Sophia Pietrovna could see the wind playing with the tails of his overcoat and with the creepers on the terrace. It was also plain how pale Ilyin was, and how he twisted his upper-lip, trying to smile. "Sonia, Sonichka, my dear little woman," he murmured, not letting her speak. "My darling, my pretty one."

In a paroxysm of tenderness with tears in his voice, he showered her with endearing words each tenderer than the other, and was already speaking to her as if she were his wife or his mistress. Suddenly and unexpectedly to her, he put one arm round her and with the other hand he seized her elbow.

"My dear one, my beauty," he began to whisper, kissing the nape of her neck; "be sincere, come to me now."

She slipped out of his embrace and lifted her head to break out in indignation and revolt. But indignation did not come, and of all her praiseworthy virtue and purity, there was left only enough for her to say that which all average women say in similar circumstances:

"You must be mad."

"But really let us go," continued Ilyin. "Just now and over there by the bench I felt convinced that you, Sonia, were as helpless as myself. You too will be all the worse for it. You love me, and you are making a useless bargain with your conscience."

Seeing that she was leaving him he seized her by her lace sleeve and ended quickly:

"If not to-day, then to-morrow; but you will have to give in. What's the good of putting if off? My dear, my darling Sonia, the verdict has been pronounced. Why postpone the execution? Why deceive yourself?"

Sophia Pietrovna broke away from him and suddenly disappeared inside the door. She returned to the drawing-room, shut the piano mechanically, stared for a long time at the cover of a music book, and sat down. She could neither stand nor think.... From her agitation and passion remained only an awful weakness mingled with laziness and tiredness. Her conscience whispered to her that she had behaved wickedly and foolishly to-night, like a madwoman; that just now she had been kissed on the terrace, and even now she had some strange sensation in her waist and in her elbow. Not a soul was in the drawing-room. Only a single candle was burning. Madame Loubianzev sat on a little round stool before the piano without stirring as if waiting for something, and as if taking advantage of her extreme exhaustion and the dark a heavy unconquerable desire began to possess her. Like a boa-constrictor, it enchained her limbs and soul. It grew every second and was no longer threatening, but stood clear before her in all its nakedness.

She sat thus for half an hour, not moving, and not stopping herself from thinking of Ilyin. Then she got up lazily and went slowly into the bed-room. Andrey Ilyitch was in bed already. She sat by the window and gave herself to her desire. She felt no more "confusion." All her feelings and thoughts pressed lovingly round some clear purpose. She still had a mind to struggle, but instantly she waved her hand impotently, realising the strength and the determination of the foe. To fight him power and strength were necessary, but her birth, up-bringing and life had given her nothing on which to lean.

"You're immoral, you're horrible," she tormented herself for her weakness. "You're a nice sort, you are!"

So indignant was her insulted modesty at this weakness that she called herself all the bad names that she knew and she related to herself many insulting, degrading truths. Thus she told herself that she never was moral, and she had not fallen before only because there was no pretext, that her day-long struggle had been nothing but a game and a comedy....

"Let us admit that I struggled," she thought, "but what kind of a fight was it? Even prostitutes struggle before they sell themselves, and still they do sell themselves. It's a pretty sort of fight. Like milk, turns in a day." She realised that it was not love that drew her from her home nor Ilyin's personality, but the sensations which await her.... A little week-end type like the rest of them.

"When the young bird's mother was killed," a hoarse tenor finished singing.

If I am going, it's time, thought Sophia Pietrovna. Her heart began to beat with a frightful force.

"Andrey," she almost cried. "Listen. Shall we go away? Shall we? Yes?"

"Yes.... I've told you already. You go alone."

"But listen," she said, "if you don't come too, you may lose me. I seem to be in love already."

"Who with?" Andrey Ilyitch asked.

"It must be all the same for you, who with," Sophia Pietrovna cried out.

Andrey Ilyitch got up, dangled his feet over the side of the bed, with a look of surprise at the dark form of his wife.

"Imagination," he yawned.

He could not believe her, but all the same he was frightened. After having thought for a while, and asked his wife some unimportant questions, he gave his views of the family, of infidelity.... He spoke sleepily for about ten minutes and then lay down again. His remarks had no success. There are a great many opinions in this world, and more than half of them belong to people who have never known misery.

In spite of the late hour, the bungalow people were still moving behind their windows. Sophia Pietrovna put on a long coat and stood for a while, thinking. She still had force of mind to say to her sleepy husband:

"Are you asleep? I'm going for a little walk. Would you like to come with me?"

That was her last hope. Receiving no answer, she walked out. It was breezy and cool. She did not feel the breeze or the darkness but walked on and on.... An irresistible power drove her, and it seemed to her that if she stopped that power would push her in the back. "You're an immoral woman," she murmured mechanically. "You're horrible."

She was choking for breath, burning with shame, did not feel her feet under her, for that which drove her along was stronger than her shame, her reason, her fear....

AFTER THE THEATRE

Nadya Zelenina had just returned with her mother from the theatre, where they had been to see a performance of "Eugene Oniegin." Entering her room, she quickly threw off her dress, loosened her hair, and sat down hurriedly in her petticoat and a white blouse to write a letter in the style of Tatiana.

"I love you,"—she wrote—"but you don't love me; no, you don't!"

The moment she had written this, she smiled.

She was only sixteen years old, and so far she had not been in love. She knew that Gorny, the officer, and Gronsdiev, the student, loved her; but now, after the theatre, she wanted to doubt their love. To be unloved and unhappy—how interesting. There is something beautiful, affecting, romantic in the fact that one loves deeply while the other is indifferent. Oniegin is interesting because he does not love at all, and Tatiana is delightful because she is very much in love; but if they loved each other equally and were happy, they would seem boring, instead.

"Don't go on protesting that you love me," Nadya wrote on, thinking of Gorny, the officer, "I can't believe you. You're very clever, educated, serious; you have a great talent, and perhaps, a splendid future waiting, but I am an uninteresting poor-spirited girl, and you yourself know quite well that I shall only be a drag upon your life. It's true I carried you off your feet, and you thought you had met your ideal in me, but that was a mistake. Already you are asking yourself in despair, 'Why did I meet this girl?' Only your kindness prevents you from confessing it."

Nadya pitied herself. She wept and went on.

"If it were not so difficult for me to leave mother and brother I would put on a nun's gown and go where my eyes direct me. You would then be free to love another. If I were to die!"

Through her tears she could not make out what she had written. Brief rainbows trembled on the table, on the floor and the ceiling, as though Nadya were looking through a prism. Impossible to write. She sank back in her chair and began to think of Gorny.

Oh, how fascinating, how interesting men are! Nadya remembered the beautiful expression of Gorny's face, appealing, guilty, and tender, when someone discussed music with him,—the efforts he made to prevent the passion from sounding in his voice. Passion must be concealed in a society where cold reserve and indifference are the signs of good breeding. And he does try to conceal it, but he does not succeed, and everybody knows quite well that he has a passion for music. Never-ending discussions about music, blundering pronouncements by men who do not understand—keep him in incessant tension. He is scared, timid, silent. He plays superbly, as an ardent pianist. If he were not an officer, he would be a famous musician.

The tears dried in her eyes. Nadya remembered how Gorny told her of his love at a symphony concert, and again downstairs by the cloak-room.

"I am so glad you have at last made the acquaintance of the student Gronsdiev," she continued to write. "He is a very clever man, and you are sure to love him. Yesterday he was sitting with us till two o'clock in the morning. We were all so happy. I was sorry that you hadn't come to us. He said a lot of remarkable things."

Nadya laid her hands on the table and lowered her head. Her hair covered the letter. She remembered that Gronsdiev also loved her, and that he had the same right to her letter as Gorny. Perhaps she had better write to Gronsdiev? For no cause, a happiness began to quicken in her breast. At first it was a little one, rolling about in her breast like a rubber ball. Then it grew broader and bigger, and broke forth like a wave. Nadya had already forgotten about Gorny and Gronsdiev. Her thoughts became confused. The happiness grew more and more. From her breast it ran into her arms and legs, and it seemed that a light fresh breeze blew over her head, stirring her hair. Her shoulders trembled with quiet laughter. The table and the lampglass trembled. Tears from her eyes splashed the letter. She was powerless to stop her laughter; and to convince herself that she had a reason for it, she hastened to remember something funny.

"What a funny poodle!" she cried, feeling that she was choking with laughter. "What a funny poodle!"

She remembered how Gronsdiev was playing with Maxim the poodle after tea yesterday; how he told a story afterwards of a very clever poodle who was chasing a crow in the yard. The crow gave him a look and said:

"Oh, you swindler!"

The poodle did not know he had to do with a learned crow. He was terribly confused, and ran away dumfounded. Afterwards he began to bark.

"No, I'd better love Gronsdiev," Nadya decided and tore up the letter.

She began to think of the student, of his love, of her own love, with the result that the thoughts in her head swam apart and she thought about everything, about her mother, the street, the pencil, the piano. She was happy thinking, and found that everything was good, magnificent. Her happiness told her that this was not all, that a little later it would be still better. Soon it will be spring, summer. They will go with mother to Gorbiki in the country. Gorny will come for his holidays. He will walk in the orchard with her, and make love to her. Gronsdiev will come too. He will play croquet with her and bowls. He will tell funny, wonderful stories. She passionately longed for the orchard, the darkness, the pure sky, the stars. Again her shoulders trembled with laughter and she seemed to awake to a smell of wormwood in the room; and a branch was tapping at the window.

She went to her bed and sat down. She did not know what to do with her great happiness. It overwhelmed her. She stared at the crucifix which hung at the head of her bed and saying:

"Dear God, dear God, dear God."

THAT WRETCHED BOY

Ivan Ivanich Lapkin, a pleasant looking young man, and Anna Zamblizky, a young girl with a little snub nose, walked down the sloping bank and sat down on the bench. The bench was close to the water's edge, among thick bushes of young willow. A heavenly spot! You sat down, and you were hidden from the world. Only the fish could see you and the catspaws which flashed over the water like lightning. The two young persons were equipped with rods, fish hooks, bags, tins of worms and everything else necessary. Once seated, they immediately began to fish.

"I am glad that we're left alone at last," said Lapkin, looking round. I've got a lot to tell you, Anna—tremendous ... when I saw you for the first time ... you've got a nibble ... I understood then—why I am alive, I knew where my idol was, to whom I can devote my honest, hardworking life.... It must be a big one ... it is biting.... When I saw you—for the first time in my life I fell in love—fell in love passionately I Don't pull. Let it go on biting.... Tell me, darling, tell me—will you let me hope? No! I'm not worth it. I dare not even think of it—may I hope for.... Pull!

Anna lifted her hand that held the rod—pulled, cried out. A silvery green fish shone in the air.

"Goodness! it's a perch! Help—quick! It's slipping off." The perch tore itself from the hook—danced in the grass towards its native element and ... leaped into the water.

But instead of the little fish that he was chasing, Lapkin quite by accident caught hold of Anna's hand—quite by accident pressed it to his lips. She drew back, but it was too late; quite by accident their lips met and kissed; yes, it was an absolute accident! They kissed and kissed. Then came vows and assurances.... Blissful moments! But there is no such thing as absolute happiness in this life. If happiness itself does not contain a poison, poison will enter in from without. Which happened this time. Suddenly, while the two were kissing, a laugh was heard. They looked at the river and were paralysed. The schoolboy Kolia, Anna's brother, was standing in the water, watching the young people and maliciously laughing.

"Ah—ha! Kissing!" said he. "Right O, I'll tell Mother."

"I hope that you—as a man of honour," Lapkin muttered, blushing. "It's disgusting to spy on us, it's loathsome to tell tales, it's rotten. As a man of honour...."

"Give me a shilling, then I'll shut up!" the man of honour retorted. "If you don't, I'll tell."

Lapkin took a shilling out of his pocket and gave it to Kolia, who squeezed it in his wet fist, whistled, and swam away. And the young people did not kiss any more just then.

Next day Lapkin brought Kolia some paints and a ball from town, and his sister gave him all her empty pill boxes. Then they had to present him with a set of studs like dogs' heads. The wretched boy enjoyed this game immensely, and to keep it going he began to spy on them. Wherever Lapkin and Anna went, he was there too. He did not leave them alone for a single moment.

"Beast!" Lapkin gnashed his teeth. "So young and yet such a full fledged scoundrel. What on earth will become of him later!"

During the whole of July the poor lovers had no life apart from him. He threatened to tell on them; he dogged them and demanded more presents. Nothing satisfied him—finally he hinted at a gold watch. All right, they had to promise the watch.

Once, at table, when biscuits were being handed round, he burst out laughing and said to Lapkin: "Shall I let on? Ah—ha!"

Lapkin blushed fearfully and instead of a biscuit he began to chew his table napkin. Anna jumped up from the table and rushed out of the room.

And this state of things went on until the end of August, up to the day when Lapkin at last proposed to Anna. Ah! What a happy day that was! When he had spoken to her parents and obtained their consent Lapkin rushed into the garden after Kolia. When he found him he nearly cried for joy and caught hold of the wretched boy by the ear. Anna, who was also looking for Kolia came running up and grabbed him by the other ear. You should have seen the happiness depicted on their faces while Kolia roared and begged them:

"Darling, precious pets, I won't do it again. O-oh—O-oh! Forgive me!" And both of them confessed afterwards that during all the time they were in love with each other they never experienced such happiness, such overwhelming joy as during those moments when they pulled the wretched boy's ears.

ENEMIES

About ten o'clock of a dark September evening the Zemstvo doctor Kirilov's only son, six-year-old Andrey, died of diphtheria. As the doctor's wife dropped on to her knees before the dead child's cot and the first paroxysm of despair took hold of her, the bell rang sharply in the hall.

When the diphtheria came all the servants were sent away from the house, that very morning. Kirilov himself went to the door, just as he was, in his shirt-sleeves with his waistcoat unbuttoned, without wiping his wet face or hands, which had been burnt with carbolic acid. It was dark in the hall, and of the person who entered could be distinguished only his middle height, a white scarf and a big, extraordinarily pale face, so pale that it seemed as though its appearance made the hall brighter....

"Is the doctor in?" the visitor asked abruptly.

"I'm at home," answered Kirilov. "What do you want?"

"Oh, you're the doctor? I'm so glad!" The visitor was overjoyed and began to seek for the doctor's hand in the darkness. He found it and squeezed it hard in his own. "I'm very ... very glad! We were introduced ... I am Aboguin ... had the pleasure of meeting you this summer at Mr. Gnouchev's. I am very glad to have found you at home.... For God's sake, don't say you won't come with me immediately.... My wife has been taken dangerously ill.... I have the carriage with me...."

From the visitor's voice and movements it was evident that he had been in a state of violent agitation. Exactly as though he had been frightened by a fire or a mad dog, he could hardly restrain his hurried breathing, and he spoke quickly in a trembling voice. In his speech there sounded a note of real sincerity, of childish fright. Like all men who are frightened and dazed, he spoke in short, abrupt phrases and uttered many superfluous, quite unnecessary, words.

"I was afraid I shouldn't find you at home," he continued. "While I was coming to you I suffered terribly.... Dress yourself and let us go, for God's sake.... It happened like this. Papchinsky came to me—Alexander Siemionovich, you know him.... We were chatting.... Then we sat down to tea. Suddenly my wife cries out, presses her hands to her heart, and falls back in her chair. We carried her off to her bed and ... and I rubbed her forehead with sal-volatile, and splashed her with water.... She lies like a corpse.... I'm afraid that her heart's failed.... Let us go.... Her father too died of heart-failure."

Kirilov listened in silence as though he did not understand the Russian language.

When Aboguin once more mentioned Papchinsky and his wife's father, and once more began to seek for the doctor's hand in the darkness, the doctor shook his head and said, drawling each word listlessly:

"Excuse me, but I can't go.... Five minutes ago my ... my son died."

"Is that true?" Aboguin whispered, stepping back. "My God, what an awful moment to come! It's a terribly fated day ... terribly! What a coincidence ... and it might have been on purpose!"

Aboguin took hold of the door handle and drooped his head in meditation. Evidently he was hesitating, not knowing whether to go away, or to ask the doctor once more.

"Listen," he said eagerly, seizing Kirilov by the sleeve. "I fully understand your state! God knows I'm ashamed to try to hold your attention at such a moment, but what can I do? Think yourself—who can I go to? There isn't another doctor here besides you. For heaven's sake come. I'm not asking for myself. It's not I that's ill!"

Silence began. Kirilov turned his back to Aboguin, stood still for a while and slowly went out of the hall into the drawing-room. To judge by his uncertain, machine-like movement, and by the attentiveness with which he arranged the hanging shade on the unlighted lamp in the drawing-room and consulted a thick book which lay on the table—at such a moment he had neither purpose nor desire, nor did he think of anything, and probably had already forgotten that there was a stranger standing in his hall. The gloom and the quiet of the drawing-room apparently increased his insanity. As he went from the drawing-room to his study he raised his right foot higher than he need, felt with his hands for the door-posts, and then one felt a certain perplexity in his whole figure, as though he had entered a strange house by chance, or for the first time in his life had got drunk, and now was giving himself up in bewilderment to the new sensation. A wide line of light stretched across the bookshelves on one wall of the study; this light, together with the heavy stifling smell of carbolic acid and ether came from the door ajar that led from the study into the bed-room.... The doctor sank into a chair before the table; for a while he looked drowsily at the shining books, then rose and went into the bed-room.

Here, in the bed-room, dead quiet reigned. Everything, down to the last trifle, spoke eloquently of the tempest undergone, of weariness, and everything rested. The candle which stood among a close crowd of phials, boxes and jars on the stool and the big lamp on the chest of drawers brightly lit the room. On the bed, by the window, the boy lay open-eyed, with a look of wonder on his face. He did not move, but it seemed that his open eyes became darker and darker every second and sank into his skull. Having laid her hands on his body and hid her face in the folds of the bed-clothes, the mother now was on her knees before the bed. Like the boy she did not move, but how much living movement was felt in the coil of her body and in her hands! She was pressing close to the bed with her whole being, with eager vehemence, as though she were afraid to violate the quiet and comfortable pose which she had found at last for her weary body. Blankets, cloths, basins, splashes on the floor, brushes and spoons scattered everywhere, a white bottle of lime-water, the stifling heavy air itself—everything died away, and as it were plunged into quietude.

The doctor stopped by his wife, thrust his hands into his trouser pockets and bending his head on one side looked fixedly at his son. His face showed indifference; only the drops which glistened on his beard revealed that he had been lately weeping.

The repulsive terror of which we think when we speak of death was absent from the bed-room. In the pervading dumbness, in the mother's pose, in the indifference of the doctor's face was something attractive that touched the heart, the subtle and elusive beauty of human grief, which it will take men long to understand and describe, and only music, it seems, is able to express. Beauty too was felt in the stern stillness. Kirilov and his wife were silent and did not weep, as though they confessed all the poetry of their condition. As once the season of their youth passed away, so now in this boy their right to bear children had passed away, alas! for ever to eternity. The doctor is forty-four years old, already grey and looks like an old man; his faded sick wife is thirty-five. Audrey was not merely the only son but the last.

In contrast to his wife the doctor's nature belonged to those which feel the necessity of movement when their soul is in pain. After standing by his wife for about five minutes, he passed from the bed-room, lifting his right foot too high, into a little room half filled with a big broad divan. From there he went to the kitchen. After wandering about the fireplace and the cook's bed, he stooped through a little door and came into the hall.

Here he saw the white scarf and the pale face again.

"At last," sighed Aboguin, seizing the doorhandle. "Let us go, please."

The doctor shuddered, glanced at him and remembered.

"Listen. I've told you already that I can't go," he said, livening. "What a strange idea!"

"Doctor, I'm made of flesh and blood, too. I fully understand your condition. I sympathise with you," Aboguin said in an imploring voice, putting his hand to his scarf. "But I am not asking for myself. My wife is dying. If you had heard her cry, if you'd seen her face, you would understand my insistence! My God—and I thought that you'd gone to dress yourself. The time is precious, Doctor! Let us go, I beg of you."

"I can't come," Kirilov said after a pause, and stepped into his drawing-room.

Aboguin followed him and seized him by the sleeve.

"You're in sorrow. I understand. But I'm not asking you to cure a toothache, or to give expert evidence,—but to save a human life." He went on imploring like a beggar. "This life is more than any personal grief. I ask you for courage, for a brave deed—in the name of humanity."

"Humanity cuts both ways," Kirilov said irritably. "In the name of the same humanity I ask you not to take me away. My God, what a strange idea! I can hardly stand on my feet and you frighten me with humanity. I'm not fit for anything now. I won't go for anything. With whom shall I leave my wife? No, no...."

Kirilov flung out his open hands and drew back.

"And ... and don't ask me," he continued, disturbed. "I'm sorry.... Under the Laws, Volume XIII., I'm obliged to go and you have the right to drag me by the neck.... Well, drag me, but ... I'm not fit.... I'm not even able to speak. Excuse me."

"It's quite unfair to speak to me in that tone, Doctor," said Aboguin, again taking the doctor by the sleeve. "The thirteenth volume be damned! I have no right to do violence to your will. If you want to, come; if you don't, then God be with you; but it's not to your will that I apply, but to your feelings. A young woman is dying! You say your son died just now. Who could understand my terror better than you?"

Aboguin's voice trembled with agitation. His tremor and his tone were much more convincing than his words. Aboguin was sincere, but it is remarkable that every phrase he used came out stilted, soulless, inopportunely florid, and as it were insulted the atmosphere of the doctor's house and the woman who was dying. He felt it himself, and in his fear of being misunderstood he exerted himself to the utmost to make his voice soft and tender so as to convince by the sincerity of his tone at least, if not by his words. As a rule, however deep and beautiful the words they affect only the unconcerned. They cannot always satisfy those who are happy or distressed because the highest expression of happiness or distress is most often silence. Lovers understand each other best when they are silent, and a fervent passionate speech at the graveside affects only outsiders. To the widow and children it seems cold and trivial.

Kirilov stood still and was silent. When Aboguin uttered some more words on the higher vocation of a doctor, and self-sacrifice, the doctor sternly asked:

"Is it far?"

"Thirteen or fourteen versts. I've got good horses, doctor. I give you my word of honour that I'll take you there and back in an hour. Only an hour."

The last words impressed the doctor more strongly than the references to humanity or the doctor's vocation. He thought for a while and said with a sigh.

"Well, let us go!"

He went off quickly, with a step that was now sure, to his study and soon after returned in a long coat. Aboguin, delighted, danced impatiently round him, helped him on with his overcoat, and accompanied him out of the house.

Outside it was dark, but brighter than in the hall. Now in the darkness the tall stooping figure of the doctor was clearly visible with the long, narrow beard and the aquiline nose. Besides his pale face Aboguin's big face could now be seen and a little student's cap which hardly covered the crown of his head. The scarf showed white only in front, but behind it was hid under his long hair.

"Believe me, I'm able to appreciate your magnanimity," murmured Aboguin, as he helped the doctor to a seat in the carriage. "We'll whirl away. Luke, dear man, drive as fast as you can, do!"

The coachman drove quickly. First appeared a row of bare buildings, which stood along the hospital yard. It was dark everywhere, save that at the end of the yard a bright light from someone's window broke through the garden fence, and three windows in the upper story of the separate house seemed to be paler than the air. Then the carriage drove into dense obscurity where you could smell mushroom damp, and hear the whisper of the trees. The noise of the wheels awoke the rooks who began to stir in the leaves and raised a doleful, bewildered cry as if they knew that the doctor's son was dead and Aboguin's wife ill. Then began to appear separate trees, a shrub. Sternly gleamed the pond, where big black shadows slept. The carriage rolled along over an even plain. Now the cry of the rooks was but faintly heard far away behind. Soon it became completely still.

Almost all the way Kirilov and Aboguin were silent; save that once Aboguin sighed profoundly and murmured.

"It's terrible pain. One never loves his nearest so much as when there is the risk of losing them."

And when the carriage was quietly passing through the river, Kirilov gave a sudden start, as though the dashing of the water frightened him, and he began to move impatiently.

"Let me go," he said in anguish. "I'll come to you later. I only want to send the attendant to my wife. She is all alone."

Aboguin was silent. The carriage, swaying and rattling against the stones, drove over the sandy bank and went on. Kirilov began to toss about in anguish, and glanced around. Behind the road was visible in the scant light of the stars and the willows that fringed the bank disappearing into the darkness. To the right the plain stretched smooth and boundless as heaven. On it in the distance here and there dim lights were burning, probably on the turf-pits. To the left, parallel with the road stretched a little hill, tufted with tiny shrubs, and on the hill a big half-moon stood motionless, red, slightly veiled with a mist, and surrounded with fine clouds which seemed to be gazing upon it from every side, and guarding it, lest it should disappear.

In all nature one felt something hopeless and sick. Like a fallen woman who sits alone in a dark room trying not to think of her past, the earth languished with reminiscence of spring and summer and waited in apathy for ineluctable winter. Wherever one's glance turned nature showed everywhere like a dark, cold, bottomless pit, whence neither Kirilov nor Aboguin nor the red half-moon could escape....

The nearer the carriage approached the destination the more impatient did Aboguin become. He moved about, jumped up and stared over the driver's shoulder in front of him. And when at last the carriage drew up at the foot of the grand staircase, nicely covered with a striped linen awning and he looked up at the lighted windows of the first floor one could hear his breath trembling.

"If anything happens ... I shan't survive it," he said entering the hall with the doctor and slowly rubbing his hands in his agitation. "But I can't hear any noise. That means it's all right so far," he added, listening to the stillness.

No voices or steps were heard in the hall. For all the bright illumination the whole house seemed asleep. Now the doctor and Aboguin who had been in darkness up till now could examine each other. The doctor was tall, with a stoop, slovenly dressed, and his face was plain. There was something unpleasantly sharp, ungracious, and severe in his thick negro lips, his aquiline nose and his faded, indifferent look. His tangled hair, his sunken temples, the early grey in his long thin beard, that showed his shining chin, his pale grey complexion and the slipshod awkwardness of his manners—the hardness of it all suggested to the mind bad times undergone, an unjust lot and weariness of life and men. To look at the hard figure of the man, you could not believe that he had a wife and could weep over his child. Aboguin revealed something different. He was robust, solid and fair-haired, with a big head and large, yet soft, features, exquisitely dressed in the latest fashion. In his carriage, his tight-buttoned coat and his mane of hair you felt something noble and leonine. He walked with his head straight and his chest prominent, he spoke in a pleasant baritone, and in his manner of removing his scarf or arranging his hair there appeared a subtle, almost feminine, elegance.

Even his pallor and childish fear as he glanced upwards to the staircase while taking off his coat, did not disturb his carriage or take from the satisfaction, the health and aplomb which his figure breathed.

"There's no one about, nothing I can hear," he said walking upstairs. "No commotion. May God be good!"

He accompanied the doctor through the hall to a large salon, where a big piano showed dark and a lustre hung in a white cover. Thence they both passed into a small and beautiful drawing-room, very cosy, filled with a pleasant, rosy half-darkness.

"Please sit here a moment, Doctor," said Aboguin, "I ... I won't be a second. I'll just have a look and tell them."

Kirilov was left alone. The luxury of the drawing-room, the pleasant half-darkness, even his presence in a stranger's unfamiliar house evidently did not move him. He sat in a chair looking at his hands burnt with carbolic acid. He had no more than a glimpse of the bright red lampshade, the cello case, and when he looked sideways across the room to where the dock was ticking, he noticed a stuffed wolf, as solid and satisfied as Aboguin himself.

It was still.... Somewhere far away in the other rooms someone uttered a loud "Ah!" A glass door, probably a cupboard door, rang, and again everything was still. After five minutes had passed, Kirilov did not look at his hands any more. He raised his eyes to the door through which Aboguin had disappeared.

Aboguin was standing on the threshold, but not the same man as went out. The expression of satisfaction and subtle elegance had disappeared from him. His face and hands, the attitude of his body were distorted with a disgusting expression either of horror or of tormenting physical pain. His nose, lips, moustache, all his features were moving and as it were trying to tear themselves away from his face, but the eyes were as though laughing from pain.

Aboguin took a long heavy step into the middle of the room, stooped, moaned, and shook his fists.

"Deceived!" he cried, emphasising the syllable cei. "She deceived me! She's gone! She fell ill and sent me for the doctor only to run away with this fool Papchinsky. My God!" Aboguin stepped heavily towards the doctor, thrust his white soft fists before his face, and went on wailing, shaking his fists the while.

"She's gone off! She's deceived me! But why this lie? My God, my God! Why this dirty, foul trick, this devilish, serpent's game? What have I done to her? She's gone off." Tears gushed from his eyes. He turned on his heel and began to pace the drawing-room. Now in his short jacket and his fashionable narrow trousers in which his legs seemed too thin for his body, he was extraordinarily like a lion. Curiosity kindled in the doctor's impassive face. He rose and eyed Aboguin.

"Well, where's the patient?"

"The patient, the patient," cried Aboguin, laughing, weeping, and still shaking his fists. "She's not ill, but accursed. Vile—dastardly. The Devil himself couldn't have planned a fouler trick. She sent me so that she could run away with a fool, an utter clown, an Alphonse! My God, far better she should have died. I'll not bear it. I shall not bear it."

The doctor stood up straight. His eyes began to blink, filled with tears; his thin beard began to move with his jaw right and left.

"What's this?" he asked, looking curiously about. "My child's dead. My wife in anguish, alone in all the house.... I can hardly stand on my feet, I haven't slept for three nights ... and I'm made to play in a vulgar comedy, to play the part of a stage property! I don't ... I don't understand it!"

Aboguin opened one fist, flung a crumpled note on the floor and trod on it, as upon an insect he wished to crush.

"And I didn't see ... didn't understand," he said through his set teeth, brandishing one fist round his head, with an expression as though someone had trod on a corn. "I didn't notice how he came to see us every day. I didn't notice that he came in a carriage to-day! What was the carriage for? And I didn't see! Innocent!"

"I don't ... I don't understand," the doctor murmured. "What's it all mean? It's jeering at a man, laughing at a man's suffering! That's impossible.... I've never seen it in my life before!"

With the dull bewilderment of a man who has just begun to understand that someone has bitterly offended him, the doctor shrugged his shoulders, waved his hands and not knowing what to say or do, dropped exhausted into a chair.

"Well, she didn't love me any more. She loved another man. Very well. But why the deceit, why this foul treachery?" Aboguin spoke with tears in his voice. "Why, why? What have I done to you? Listen, doctor," he said passionately approaching Kirilov. "You were the unwilling witness of my misfortune, and I am not going to hide the truth from you. I swear I loved this woman. I loved her with devotion, like a slave. I sacrificed everything for her. I broke with my family, I gave up the service and my music. I forgave her things I could not have forgiven my mother and sister.... I never once gave her an angry look ... I never gave her any cause. Why this lie then? I do not demand love, but why this abominable deceit? If you don't love any more then speak out honestly, above all when you know what I feel about this matter...."

With tears in his eyes and trembling in all his bones, Aboguin was pouring out his soul to the doctor. He spoke passionately, pressing both hands to his heart. He revealed all the family secrets without hesitation, as though he were glad that these secrets were being tom from his heart. Had he spoken thus for an hour or two and poured out all his soul, he would surely have been easier.

Who can say whether, had the doctor listened and given him friendly sympathy, he would not, as so often happens, have been reconciled to his grief unprotesting, without turning to unprofitable follies? But it happened otherwise. While Aboguin was speaking the offended doctor changed countenance visibly. The indifference and amazement in his face gradually gave way to an expression of bitter outrage, indignation, and anger. His features became still sharper, harder, and more forbidding. When Aboguin put before his eyes the photograph of his young wife, with a pretty, but dry, inexpressive face like a nun's, and asked if it were possible to look at that face and grant that it could express a lie, the doctor suddenly started away, with flashing eyes, and said, coarsely forging out each several word:

"Why do you tell me all this? I do not want to hear! I don't want to," he cried and banged his fist upon the table. "I don't want your trivial vulgar secrets—to Hell with them. You dare not tell me such trivialities. Or do you think I have not yet been insulted enough! That I'm a lackey to whom you can give the last insult? Yes?"

Aboguin drew back from Kirilov and stared at him in surprise.

"Why did you bring me here?" the doctor went on, shaking his beard. "You marry out of high spirits, get angry out of high spirits, and make a melodrama—but where do I come in? What have I got to do with your romances? Leave me alone I Get on with your noble grabbing, parade your humane ideas, play—" the doctor gave a side-glance at the cello-case—"the double-bass and the trombone, stuff yourselves like capons, but don't dare to jeer at a real man! If you can't respect him, then you can at least spare him your attentions."

"What does all this mean?" Aboguin asked, blushing.

"It means that it's vile and foul to play with a man I I'm a doctor. You consider doctors and all men who work and don't reek of scent and harlotry, your footmen, your mauvais tons. Very well, but no one gave you the right to turn a man who suffers into a property."

"How dare you say that?" Aboguin asked quietly. Again his face began to twist about, this time in visible anger.

"How dare you bring me here to listen to trivial rubbish, when you know that I'm in sorrow?" the doctor cried and banged his fists on the table once more. "Who gave you the right to jeer at another's grief?"

"You're mad," cried Aboguin. "You're ungenerous. I too am deeply unhappy and ... and ..."

"Unhappy"—the doctor gave a sneering laugh—"Don't touch the word, it's got nothing to do with you. Wasters who can't get money on a bill call themselves unhappy too. A capon's unhappy, oppressed with all its superfluous fat. You worthless lot!"

"Sir, you're forgetting yourself," Aboguin gave a piercing scream. "For words like those, people are beaten. Do you understand?"

Aboguin thrust his hand into his side pocket, took out a pocket-book, found two notes and flung them on the table.

"There's your fee," he said, and his nostrils trembled. "You're paid."

"You dare not offer me money," said the doctor, and brushed the notes from the table to the floor. "You don't settle an insult with money."

Aboguin and the doctor stood face to face, heaping each other with undeserved insults. Never in their lives, even in a frenzy, had they said so much that was unjust and cruel and absurd. In both the selfishness of the unhappy is violently manifest. Unhappy men are selfish, wicked, unjust, and less able to understand each other than fools. Unhappiness does not unite people, but separates them; and just where one would imagine that people should be united by the community of grief, there is more injustice and cruelty done than among the comparatively contented.

"Send me home, please," the doctor cried, out of breath.

Aboguin rang the bell violently. Nobody came. He rang once more; then flung the bell angrily to the floor. It struck dully on the carpet and gave out a mournful sound like a death-moan. The footman appeared.

"Where have you been hiding, damn you?" The master sprang upon him with clenched fists. "Where have you been just now? Go away and tell them to said the carriage round for this gentleman, and get the brougham ready for me. Wait," he called out as the footman turned to go. "Not a single traitor remains to-morrow. Pack off all of you! I will engage new ones ... Rabble!"

While they waited Aboguin and the doctor were silent. Already the expression of satisfaction and the subtle elegance had returned to the former. He paced the drawing-room, shook his head elegantly and evidently was planning something. His anger was not yet cool, but he tried to make as if he did not notice his enemy.... The doctor stood with one hand on the edge of the table, looking at Aboguin with that deep, rather cynical, ugly contempt with which only grief and an unjust lot can look, when they see satiety and elegance before them.

A little later, when the doctor took his seat in the carriage and drove away, his eyes still glanced contemptuously. It was dark, much darker than an hour ago. The red half-moon had now disappeared behind the little hill, and the clouds which watched it lay in dark spots round the stars. The brougham with the red lamps began to rattle on the road and passed the doctor. It was Aboguin on his way to protest, to commit all manner of folly.

All the way the doctor thought not of his wife or Andrey, but only of Aboguin and those who lived in the house he just left. His thoughts were unjust, inhuman, and cruel. He passed sentence on Aboguin, his wife, Papchinsky, and all those who live in rosy semi-darkness and smell of scent. All the way he hated them, and his heart ached with his contempt for them. The conviction he formed about them would last his life long.

Time will pass and Kirilov's sorrow, but this conviction, unjust and unworthy of the human heart, will not pass, but will remain in the doctor's mind until the grave.

A TRIFLING OCCURRENCE

Nicolai Ilyich Byelyaev, a Petersburg landlord, very fond of the racecourse, a well fed, pink young man of about thirty-two, once called towards evening on Madame Irnin—Olga Ivanovna—with whom he had a liaison, or, to use his own phrase, spun out a long and tedious romance. And indeed the first pages of this romance, pages of interest and inspiration, had been read long ago; now they dragged on and on, and presented neither novelty nor interest.

Finding that Olga Ivanovna was not at home, my hero lay down a moment on the drawing-room sofa and began to wait.

"Good evening, Nicolai Ilyich," he suddenly heard a child's voice say. "Mother will be in in a moment. She's gone to the dressmaker's with Sonya."

In the same drawing-room on the sofa lay Olga Vassilievna's son, Alyosha, a boy about eight years old, well built, well looked after, dressed up like a picture in a velvet jacket and long black stockings. He lay on a satin pillow, and apparently imitating an acrobat whom he had lately seen in the circus, lifted up first one leg then the other. When his elegant legs began to be tired, he moved his hands, or he jumped up impetuously and then went on all fours, trying to stand with his legs in the air. All this he did with a most serious face, breathing heavily, as if he himself found no happiness in God's gift of such a restless body.

"Ah, how do you do, my friend?" said Byelyaev. "Is it you? I didn't notice you. Is your mother well?"

At the moment Alyosha had just taken hold of the toe of his left foot in his right hand and got into a most awkward pose. He turned head over heels, jumped up, and glanced from under the big, fluffy lampshade at Byelyaev.

"How can I put it?" he said, shrugging his shoulders. "As a matter of plain fact mother is never well. You see she's a woman, and women, Nicolai Ilyich, have always some pain or another."

For something to do, Byelyaev began to examine Alyosha's face. All the time he had been acquainted with Olga Ivanovna he had never once turned his attention to the boy and had completely ignored his existence. A boy is stuck in front of your eyes, but what is he doing here, what is his rôle?—you don't want to give a single thought to the question.

In the evening dusk Alyosha's face with a pale forehead and steady black eyes unexpectedly reminded Byelyaev of Olga Vassilievna as she was in the first pages of the romance. He had the desire to be affectionate to the boy.

"Come here, whipper-snapper," he said. "Come and let me have a good look at you, quite close."

The boy jumped off the sofa and ran to Byelyaev.

"Well?" Nicolai Ilyich began, putting his hand on the thin shoulders. "And how are things with you?"

"How shall I put it?... They used to be much better before."

"How?"

"Quite simple. Before, Sonya and I only had to do music and reading, and now we're given French verses to learn. You've had your hair cut lately?"

"Yes, just lately."

"That's why I noticed it. Your beard's shorter. May I touch it ... doesn't it hurt?"

"No, not a bit."

"Why is it that it hurts if you pull one hair, and when you pull a whole lot, it doesn't hurt a bit? Ah, ah I You know it's a pity you don't have side-whiskers. You should shave here, and at the sides ... and leave the hair just here."

The boy pressed close to Byelyaev and began to play with his watch-chain.

"When I go to the gymnasium," he said, "Mother is going to buy me a watch. I'll ask her to buy me a chain just like this. What a fine locket I Father has one just the same, but yours has stripes, here, and his has got letters.... Inside it's mother's picture. Father has another chain now, not in links, but like a ribbon...."

"How do you know? Do you see your father?"

"I? Mm ... no ... I ..."

Alyosha blushed and in the violent confusion of being detected in a lie began to scratch the locket busily with his finger-nail. Byelyaev looked steadily at his face and asked:

"Do you see your father?"

"No ... no!"

"But, be honest—on your honour. By your face I can see you're not telling me the truth. If you made a slip of the tongue by mistake, what's the use of shuffling. Tell me, do you see him? As one friend to another."

Alyosha mused.

"And you won't tell Mother?" he asked.

"What next."

"On your word of honour."

"My word of honour."

"Swear an oath."

"What a nuisance you are! What do you take me for?"

Alyosha looked round, made big eyes and began to whisper.

"Only for God's sake don't tell Mother! Never tell it to anyone at all, because it's a secret. God forbid that Mother should ever get to know; then I and Sonya and Pelagueia will pay for it.... Listen. Sonya and I meet Father every Tuesday and Friday. When Pelagueia takes us for a walk before dinner, we go into Apfel's sweet-shop and Father's waiting for us. He always sits in a separate room, you know, where there's a splendid marble table and an ash-tray shaped like a goose without a back...."

"And what do you do there?"

"Nothing!—First, we welcome one another, then we sit down at a little table and Father begins to treat us to coffee and cakes. You know, Sonya eats meat-pies, and I can't bear pies with meat in them! I like them made of cabbage and eggs. We eat so much that afterwards at dinner we try to eat as much as we possibly can so that Mother shan't notice."

"What do you talk about there?"

"To Father? About anything. He kisses us and cuddles us, tells us all kinds of funny stories. You know, he says that he will take us to live with him when we are grown up. Sonya doesn't want to go, but I say 'Yes.' Of course, it'll be lonely without Mother; but I'll write letters to her. How funny: we could go to her for our holidays then—couldn't we? Besides, Father says that he'll buy me a horse. He's a splendid man. I can't understand why Mother doesn't invite him to live with her or why she says we mustn't meet him. He loves Mother very much indeed. He's always asking us how she is and what she's doing. When she was ill, he took hold of his head like this ... and ran, ran, all the time. He is always telling us to obey and respect her. Tell me, is it true that we're unlucky?"

"H'm ... how?"

"Father says so. He says: 'You are unlucky children.' It's quite strange to listen to him. He says: 'You are unhappy, I'm unhappy, and Mother's unhappy.' He says: 'Pray to God for yourselves and for her.'" Alyosha's eyes rested upon the stuffed bird and he mused.

"Exactly...." snorted Byelyaev. "This is what you do. You arrange conferences in sweet-shops. And your mother doesn't know?" "N—no.... How could she know? Pelagueia won't tell for anything. The day before yesterday Father stood us pears. Sweet, like jam. I had two."

"H'm ... well, now ... tell me, doesn't your father speak about me?"

"About you? How shall I put it?" Alyosha gave a searching glance to Byelyaev's face and shrugged his shoulders.

"He doesn't say anything in particular."

"What does he say, for instance?"

"You won't be offended?"

"What next? Why, does he abuse me?"

"He doesn't abuse you, but you know ... he is cross with you. He says that it's through you that Mother's unhappy and that you ... ruined Mother. But he is so queer! I explain to him that you are good and never shout at Mother, but he only shakes his head."

"Does he say those very words: that I ruined her?"

"Yes. Don't be offended, Nicolai Ilyich!"

Byelyaev got up, stood still a moment, and then began to walk about the drawing-room.

"This is strange, and ... funny," he murmured, shrugging his shoulders and smiling ironically. "He is to blame all round, and now

I've ruined her, eh? What an innocent lamb! Did he say those very words to you: that I ruined your mother?"

"Yes, but ... you said that you wouldn't get offended."

"I'm not offended, and ... and it's none of your business! No, it ... it's quite funny though. I fell, into the trap, yet I'm to be blamed as well."

The bell rang. The boy dashed from his place and ran out. In a minute a lady entered the room with a little girl. It was Olga Ivanovna, Alyosha's mother. After her, hopping, humming noisily, and waving his hands, followed Alyosha.

"Of course, who is there to accuse except me?" he murmured, sniffing. "He's right, he's the injured husband."

"What's the matter?" asked Olga Ivanovna.

"What's the matter! Listen to the kind of sermon your dear husband preaches. It appears I'm a scoundrel and a murderer, I've ruined you and the children. All of you are unhappy, and only I am awfully happy! Awfully, awfully happy!"

"I don't understand, Nicolai! What is it?"

"Just listen to this young gentleman," Byelyaev said, pointing to Alyosha.

Alyosha blushed, then became pale suddenly and his whole face was twisted in fright.

"Nicolai Ilyich," he whispered loudly. "Shh!"

Olga Ivanovna glanced in surprise at Alyosha, at Byelyaev, and then again at Alyosha.

"Ask him, if you please," went on Byelyaev. "That stupid fool Pelagueia of yours, takes them to sweet-shops and arranges meetings with their dear father there. But that's not the point. The point is that the dear father is a martyr, and I'm a murderer, I'm a scoundrel, who broke the lives of both of you...."

"Nicolai Ilyich!" moaned Alyosha. "You gave your word of honour!"

"Ah, let me alone!" Byelyaev waved his hand. "This is something more important than any words of honour. The hypocrisy revolts me, the lie!"

"I don't understand," muttered Olga Ivanovna, and tears began to glimmer in her eyes. "Tell me, Lyolka,"—she turned to her son, "Do you see your father?"

Alyosha did not hear and looked with horror at Byelyaev.

"It's impossible," said the mother. "I'll go and ask Pelagueia."

Olga Ivanovna went out.

"But, but you gave me your word of honour," Alyosha said trembling all over.

Byelyaev waved his hand at him and went on walking up and down. He was absorbed in his insult, and now, as before, he did not notice the presence of the boy. He, a big serious man, had nothing to do with boys. And Alyosha sat down in a corner and in terror told Sonya how he had been deceived. He trembled, stammered, wept. This was the first time in his life that he had been set, roughly, face to face with a lie. He had never known before that in this world besides sweet pears and cakes and expensive watches, there exist many other things which have no name in children's language.

A GENTLEMAN FRIEND

When she came out of the hospital the charming Vanda, or, according to her passport, "the honourable lady-citizen Nastasya Kanavkina," found herself in a position in which she had never been before: without a roof and without a son. What was to be done?

First of all, she went to a pawnshop to pledge her turquoise ring, her only jewellery. They gave her a rouble for the ring ... but what can you buy for a rouble? For that you can't get a short jacket à la mode, or an elaborate hat, or a pair of brown shoes; yet without these things she felt naked. She felt as though, not only the people, but even the horses and dogs were staring at her and laughing at the plainness of her clothes. And her only thought was for her clothes; she did not care at all what she ate or where she slept.

"If only I were to meet a gentleman friend...." she thought. "I could get some money ... Nobody would say 'No,' because...."

But she came across no gentleman Mends. It's easy to find them of nights in the Renaissance, but they wouldn't let her go into the Renaissance in that plain dress and without a hat. What's to be done? After a long time of anguish, vexed and weary with walking, sitting, and thinking, Vanda made up her mind to play her last card: to go straight to the rooms of some gentleman friend and ask him for money.

"But who shall I go to?" she pondered. "I can't possibly go to Misha... he's got a family.... The ginger-headed old man is at his office...."

Vanda recollected Finkel, the dentist, the converted Jew, who gave her a bracelet three months ago. Once she poured a glass of beer on his head at the German dub. She was awfully glad that she had thought of Finkel.

"He'll be certain to give me some, if only I find him in..." she thought, on her way to him. "And if he won't, then I'll break every single thing there."

She had her plan already prepared. She approached the dentist's door. She would run up the stairs, with a laugh, fly into his private room and ask for twenty-five roubles.... But when she took hold of the bell-pull, the plan went clean out of her head. Vanda suddenly began to be afraid and agitated, a thing which had never happened to her before. She was never anything but bold and independent in drunken company; but now, dressed in common clothes, and just like any ordinary person begging a favour, she felt timid and humble.

"Perhaps he has forgotten me..." she thought, not daring to pull the bell. "And how can I go up to him in a dress like this? As if I were a pauper, or a dowdy respectable..."

She rang the bell irresolutely.

There were steps behind the door. It was the porter.

"Is the doctor at home?" she asked.

She would have been very pleased now if the porter had said "No," but instead of answering he showed her into the hall, and took her jacket. The stairs seemed to her luxurious and magnificent, but what she noticed first of all in all the luxury was a large mirror in which she saw a ragged creature without an elaborate hat, without a modish jacket, and without a pair of brown shoes. And Vanda found it strange that, now that she was poorly dressed and looking more like a seamstress or a washerwoman, for the first time she felt ashamed, and had no more assurance or boldness left. In her thoughts she began to call herself Nastya Kanavkina, instead of Vanda as she used.

"This way, please!" said the maid-servant, leading her to the private room. "The doctor will be here immediately.... Please, take a seat."

Vanda dropped into an easy chair.

"I'll say: 'Lend me ...'" she thought. "That's the right thing, because we are acquainted. But the maid must go out of the room.... It's awkward in front of the maid.... What is she standing there for?"

In five minutes the door opened and Finkel entered—a tall, swarthy, convert Jew, with fat cheeks and goggle-eyes. His cheeks, eyes, belly, fleshy hips—were all so full, repulsive, and coarse! At the Renaissance and the German club he used always to be a little drunk, to spend a lot of money on women, patiently put up with all their tricks—for instance, when Vanda poured the beer on his head, he only smiled and shook his finger at her—but now he looked dull and sleepy; he had the pompous, chilly expression of a superior, and he was chewing something.

"What is the matter?" he asked, without looking at Vanda. Vanda glanced at the maid's serious face, at the blown-out figure of Finkel, who obviously did not recognise her, and she blushed.

"What's the matter?" the dentist repeated, irritated.

"To ... oth ache...." whispered Vanda.

"Ah ... which tooth ... where?"

Vanda remembered she had a tooth with a hole.

"At the bottom ... to the right," she said.

"H'm ... open your mouth."

Finkel frowned, held his breath, and began to work the aching tooth loose.

"Do you feel any pain?" he asked, picking at her tooth with some instrument.

"Yes, I do...." Vanda lied. "Shall I remind him?" she thought, "he'll be sure to remember.... But ... the maid ... what is she standing there for?"

Finkel suddenly snorted like a steam-engine straight into her mouth, and said:

"I don't advise you to have a stopping.... Anyhow the tooth is quite useless."

Again he picked at the tooth for a little, and soiled Vanda's lips and gums with his tobacco-stained fingers. Again he held his breath and dived into her mouth with something cold....

Vanda suddenly felt a terrible pain, shrieked and seized Finkel's hand....

"Never mind...." he murmured. "Don't be frightened.... This tooth isn't any use."

And his tobacco-stained fingers, covered with blood, held up the extracted tooth before her eyes. The maid came forward and put a bowl to her lips.

"Rinse your mouth with cold water at home," said Finkel. "That will make the blood stop."

He stood before her in the attitude of a man impatient to be left alone at last.

"Good-bye ..." she said, turning to the door.

"H'm! And who's to pay me for the work?" Finkel asked laughingly.

"Ah ... yes!" Vanda recollected, blushed and gave the dentist the rouble she had got for the turquoise ring.

When she came into the street she felt still more ashamed than before, but she was not ashamed of her poverty any more. Nor did she notice any more that she hadn't an elaborate hat or a modish jacket. She walked along the street spitting blood and each red spittle told her about her life, a bad, hard life; about the insults she had suffered and had still to suffer-to-morrow, a week, a year hence—her whole life, till death....

"Oh, how terrible it is!" she whispered. "My God, how terrible!"

But the next day she was at the Renaissance and she danced there. She wore a new, immense red hat, a new jacket à la mode and a pair of brown shoes. She was treated to supper by a young merchant from Kazan.

OVERWHELMING SENSATIONS

This happened not so very long ago in the Moscow Circuit Court. The jurymen, left in court for the night, before going to bed, began a conversation about overwhelming sensations. It was occasioned by someone's recollection of a witness who became a stammerer and turned grey, owing, as he said, to one dreadful moment. The jurymen decided before going to bed that each one of them should dig into his memories and tell a story. Life is short; but still there is not a single man who can boast that he had not had some dreadful moments in his past.

One juryman related how he was nearly drowned. A second told how one night he poisoned his own child, in a place where there was neither doctor nor chemist, by giving the child white copperas in mistake for soda. The child did not die, but the father nearly went mad. A third, not an old man, but sickly, described his two attempts to commit suicide. Once he shot himself; the second time he threw himself in front of a train.

The fourth, a short, stout man, smartly dressed, told the following story:

"I was no more than twenty-two or twenty-three years old, when I fell head over heels in love with my present wife and proposed to her. Now, I would gladly give myself a thrashing for that early marriage; but then—well, I don't know what would have happened to me if Natasha had refused. My love was most ardent, the kind described in novels as mad, passionate, and so on. My happiness choked me, and I did not know how to escape from it. I bored my father, my friends, the servants by continually telling them how desperately I was in love. Happy people are quite the most tiresome and boring. I used to be awfully exasperating. Even now I'm ashamed.

"At the time I had a newly-called barrister among my friends. The barrister is now known all over Russia, but then he was only at the beginning of his popularity, and he was not rich or famous enough to have the right not to recognise a friend when he met him or not to raise his hat. I used to go and see him once or twice a week.

"When I came, we used both to stretch ourselves upon the sofas and begin to philosophise.

"Once I lay on the sofa, harping on the theme that there is no more ungrateful profession than a barrister's. I tried to show that after the witnesses have been heard the Court can easily dispense with the Crown Prosecutor and the barrister, because they are equally unnecessary and only hindrances. If an adult juryman, sound in spirit and mind, is convinced that this ceiling is white, or that Ivanov is guilty, no Demosthenes has the power to fight and overcome his conviction. Who can convince me that my moustache is carroty when I know it is black? When I listen to an orator I may perhaps get sentimental and even shed a tear, but my rooted convictions, for the most part based on the obvious and on facts, will not be changed an atom. My friend the barrister contended that I was still young and silly and was talking childish nonsense. In his opinion an obvious fact when illumined by conscientious experts became still more obvious. That was his first point. His second was that a talent is a force, an elemental power, a hurricane, that is able to turn even stones to dust, not to speak of such trifles as the convictions of householders and small shopkeepers. It is as hard for human frailty to struggle against a talent as it is to look at the sun without being blinded or to stop the wind. By the power of the word one single mortal converts thousands of convinced savages to Christianity. Ulysses was the most convinced person in the world, but he was all submission before the Syrens, and so on. All history is made up of such instances. In life we meet them at every turn. And so it ought to be; otherwise a clever person of talent would not be preferred before the stupid and untalented.

"I persisted and continued to argue that a conviction is stronger than any talent, though, speaking frankly, I myself could not define what exactly is a conviction and what is a talent. Probably I talked only for the sake of talking.

"'Take even your own case' ... said the barrister. 'You are convinced that your fiancée is an angel and that there's not a man in all the town happier than you. I tell you, ten or twenty minutes would be quite enough for me to make you sit down at this very table and write to break off the engagement.'

"I began to laugh.

"'Don't laugh. I'm talking seriously,' said my friend. 'If I only had the desire, in twenty minutes you would be happy in the thought that you have been saved from marriage. My talent is not great, but neither are you strong?'

"'Well, try, please,' I said.

"'No, why should I? I only said it in passing. You're a good boy. It would be a pity to expose you to such an experiment. Besides, I'm not in the mood, to-day.'

"We sat down to supper. The wine and thoughts of Natasha and my love utterly filled me with a sense of youth and happiness. My happiness was so infinitely great that the green-eyed barrister opposite me seemed so unhappy, so little, so grey!"

"'But do try,' I pressed him. 'I beg you.'

"The barrister shook his head and knit his brows. Evidently I had begun to bore him.

"'I know,' he said, 'that when the experiment is over you will thank me and call me saviour, but one must think of your sweetheart too. She loves you, and your refusal would make her suffer. But what a beauty she is 'I envy you.'

"The barrister sighed, swallowed some wine, and began to speak of what a wonderful creature my Natasha was. He had an uncommon gift for description. He could pour out a whole heap of words about a woman's eyelashes or her little finger. I listened to him with delight.

"'I've seen many women in my life-time;' he said, 'but I give you my word of honour, I tell you as a friend, your Natasha Andreevna is a gem, a rare girl! Of course, there are defects, even a good many, I grant you, but still she is charming.'

"And the barrister began to speak of the defects of my sweetheart. Now I quite understand it was a general conversation about women, one about their weak points in general; but it appeared to me then as though he was speaking only of Natasha. He went into raptures about her snub-nose, her excited voice, her shrill laugh, her affectation—indeed, about everything I particularly disliked in her. All this was in his opinion infinitely amiable, gracious and feminine. Imperceptibly he changed from enthusiasm first to paternal edification, then to a light, sneering tone.... There was no Chairman of the Bench with us to stop the barrister riding the high horse. I hadn't a chance of opening my mouth—and what could I have said? My friend said nothing new, his truths were long familiar. The poison was not at all in what he said, but altogether in the devilish form in which he said it. A form of Satan's own invention! As I listened to him I was convinced that one and the same word had a thousand meanings and nuances according to the way it is pronounced and the turn given to the sentence. I certainly cannot reproduce the tone or the form. I can only say that as I listened to my friend and paced from corner to corner of my room, I was revolted, exasperated, contemptuous according as he felt. I even believed him when, with tears in his eyes, he declared to me that I was a great man, deserving a better fate, and destined in the future to accomplish some remarkable exploit, from which I might be prevented by my marriage.

"'My dear friend,' he exclaimed, firmly grasping my hand, 'I implore you, I command you: stop before it is too late. Stop! God save you from this strange and terrible mistake! My friend, don't ruin your youth.'

"Believe me or not as you will, but finally I sat down at the table and wrote to my sweetheart breaking off the engagement. I wrote and rejoiced that there was still time to repair my mistake. When the envelope was sealed I hurried into the street to put it in a pillar box. The barrister came with me.

"'Splendid! Superb!' he praised me when my letter to Natasha disappeared into the darkness of the pillar-box. 'I congratulate you with all my heart. I'm delighted for your sake.'

"After we had gone about ten steps together, the barrister continued:

"'Of course, marriage has its bright side too. I, for instance, belong to the kind of men for whom marriage and family life are everything.'

"He was already describing his life: all the ugliness of a lonely bachelor existence appeared before me.

"He spoke with enthusiasm of his future wife, of the pleasures of an ordinary family life, and his transports were so beautiful and sincere that I was in absolute despair by the time we reached his door.

"'What are you doing with me, you damnable man?' I said panting. 'You've ruined me! Why did you make me write that cursed letter? I love her! I love her!'

"And I swore that I was in love. I was terrified of my action. It already seemed wild and absurd to me. Gentlemen, it is quite impossible to imagine a more overwhelming sensation than mine at that moment! If a kind man had happened to slip a revolver into my hand I would have put a bullet through my head gladly.

"'Well, that's enough, enough!' the advocate said, patting my shoulder and beginning to laugh. 'Stop crying! The letter won't reach your sweetheart. It was I, not you, wrote the address on the envelope, and I muddled it up so that they won't be able to make anything of it at the post-office. But let this be a lesson to you. Don't discuss things you don't understand.'"

"Now, gentlemen, next, please."

The fifth juryman had settled himself comfortably and already opened his mouth to begin his story, when we heard the dock striking from Spaisky Church-tower.

"Twelve...." one of the jurymen counted. "To which class, gentlemen, would you assign the sensations which our prisoner at the bar is now feeling? The murderer passes the night here in a prisoner's cell, either lying or sitting, certainly without sleeping and all through the sleepless night listens to the striking of the hours. What does he think of? What dreams visit him?"

And all the jurymen suddenly forgot about overwhelming sensations. The experience of their friend, who once wrote the letter to his Natasha, seemed unimportant, and not even amusing. Nobody told any more stories; but they began to go to bed quietly, in silence.

EXPENSIVE LESSONS

It is a great bore for an educated person not to know foreign languages. Vorotov felt it strongly, when on leaving the university after he had got his degree he occupied himself with a little scientific research.

"It's awful!" he used to say, losing his breath (for although only twenty-six he was stout, heavy, and short of breath). "It's awful. Without knowing languages I'm like a bird without wings. I'll simply have to chuck the work."

So he decided, come what might, to conquer his natural laziness and to study French and German, and he began to look out for a teacher.

One winter afternoon, as Vorotov sat working in his study, the servant announced a lady to see him.

"Show her in," said Vorotov.

And a young lady, exquisitely dressed in the latest fashion, entered the study. She introduced herself as Alice Ossipovna Enquette, a teacher of French, and said that a friend of Vorotov's had sent her to him.

"Very glad! Sit down!" said Vorotov, losing his breath, and clutching at the collar of his night shirt. (He always worked in a night shirt in order to breathe more easily.) "You were sent to me by Peter Sergueyevich? Yes.... Yes ... I asked him.... Very glad!"

While he discussed the matter with Mademoiselle Enquette he glanced at her shyly, with curiosity. She was a genuine Frenchwoman, very elegant, and still quite young. From her pale and languid face, from her short, curly hair and unnaturally small waist, you would not think her more than eighteen, but looking at her broad, well-developed shoulders, her charming back and severe eyes, Vorotov decided that she was certainly not less than twenty-three, perhaps even twenty-five; but then again it seemed to him that she was only eighteen. Her face had the cold, business-like expression of one who had come to discuss a business matter. Never once did she smile or frown, and only once a look of perplexity flashed into her eyes, when she discovered that she was not asked to teach children but a grown up, stout young man.

"So, Alice Ossipovna," Vorotov said to her, "you will give me a lesson daily from seven to eight o'clock in the evening. With regard to your wish to receive a rouble a lesson, I have no objection at all. A rouble—well, let it be a rouble...."

And he went on asking her if she wanted tea or coffee, if the weather was fine, and, smiling good naturedly, stroking the tablecloth with the palm of his hand, he asked her kindly who she was, where she had completed her education, and how she earned her living.

In a cold, business-like tone Alice Ossipovna answered that she had completed her education at a private school, and had then qualified as a domestic teacher, that her father had died recently of scarlet fever, her mother was alive and made artificial flowers, that she, Mademoiselle Enquette, gave private lessons at a pension in the morning, and from one o'clock right until the evening she taught in respectable private houses.

She went, leaving a slight and almost imperceptible perfume of a woman's dress behind her. Vorotov did not work for a long time afterwards but sat at the table stroking the green cloth and thinking.

"It's very pleasant to see girls earning their own living," he thought. "On the other hand it is very unpleasant to realise that poverty does not spare even such elegant and pretty girls as Alice Ossipovna; she, too, must struggle for her existence. Rotten luck!..."

Having never seen virtuous Frenchwomen he also thought that this exquisitely dressed Alice Ossipovna, with her well-developed shoulders and unnaturally small waist was in all probability, engaged in something else besides teaching.

Next evening when the clock pointed to five minutes to seven, Alice Ossipovna arrived, rosy from the cold; she opened Margot (an elementary text-book) and began without any preamble:

"The French grammar has twenty-six letters. The first is called A, the second B...."

"Pardon," interrupted Vorotov, smiling, "I must warn you, Mademoiselle, that you will have to change your methods somewhat in my case. The fact is that I know Russian, Latin and Greek very well. I have studied comparative philology, and it seems to me that we may leave out Margot and begin straight off to read some author." And he explained to the Frenchwoman how grown-up people study languages.

"A friend of mine," said he, "who wished to know modern languages put a French, German and Latin gospel in front of him and then minutely analysed one word after another. The result—he achieved his purpose in less than a year. Let us take some author and start reading."

The Frenchwoman gave him a puzzled look. It was evident that Vorotov's proposal appeared to her naive and absurd. If he had not been grown up she would certainly have got angry and stormed at him, but as he was a very stout, adult man at whom she could not storm, she only shrugged her shoulders half-perceptibly and said:

"Just as you please."

Vorotov ransacked his bookshelves and produced a ragged French book.

"Will this do?" he asked.

"It's all the same."

"In that case let us begin. Let us start from the title, Mémoires."

"Reminiscences...." translated Mademoiselle Enquette.

"Reminiscences...." repeated Vorotov.

Smiling good naturedly and breathing heavily, he passed a quarter of an hour over the word mémoires and the same with the word de. This tired Alice Ossipovna out. She answered his questions carelessly, got confused and evidently neither understood her pupil nor tried to. Vorotov asked her questions, and at the same time glanced furtively at her fair hair, thinking:

"The hair is not naturally curly. She waves it. Marvellous! She works from morning till night and yet she finds time to wave her hair."

At eight o'clock sharp she got up, gave him a dry, cold "Au revoir, Monsieur," and left the study. After her lingered the same sweet, subtle, agitating perfume. The pupil again did nothing for a long time, but sat by the table and thought.

During the following days he became convinced that his teacher was a charming girl serious and punctual, but very uneducated and incapable of teaching grown up people; so he decided he would not waste his time, but part with her and engage someone else. When she came for the seventh lesson he took an envelope containing seven roubles out of his pocket. Holding it in his hands and blushing furiously, he began:

"I am sorry, Alice Ossipovna, but I must tell you.... I am placed in an awkward position...."

The Frenchwoman glanced at the envelope and guessed what was the matter. For the first time during the lessons a shiver passed over her face and the cold, business-like expression disappeared. She reddened faintly, and casting her eyes down, began to play absently with her thin gold chain. And Vorotov, noticing her confusion, understood how precious this rouble was to her, how hard it would be for her to lose this money.

"I must tell you," he murmured, getting still more confused. His heart gave a thump. Quickly he put the envelope back into his pocket and continued:

"Excuse me. I ... I will leave you for ten minutes...."

And as though he did not want to dismiss her at all, but had only asked permission to retire for a moment he went into another room and sat there for ten minutes. Then he returned, more confused than ever; he thought that his leaving her like that would be explained by her in a certain way and this made him awkward.

The lessons began again.

Vorotov wanted them no more. Knowing that they would lead to nothing he gave the Frenchwoman a free hand; he did not question or interrupt her any more. She translated at her own sweet will, ten pages a lesson, but he did not listen. He breathed heavily and for want of occupation gazed now and then at her curly little head, her neck, her soft white hands, and inhaled the perfume of her dress.

He caught himself thinking about her as he ought not and it shamed him, or admiring her, and then he felt aggrieved and angry because she behaved so coldly towards him, in such a businesslike way, never smiling and as if afraid that he might suddenly touch her. All the while he thought: How could he inspire her with confidence in him, how could he get to know her better, to help her, to make her realise how badly she taught, poor little soul?

Once Alice Ossipovna came to the lesson in a dainty pink dress, a little décolleté, and such a sweet scent came from her that you might have thought she was wrapped in a cloud, that you had only to blow on her for her to fly away or dissolve like smoke. She apologised, saying she could only stay for half an hour, because she had to go straight from the lesson to a ball.

He gazed at her neck, at her bare shoulders and he thought he understood why Frenchwomen were known to be light-minded and easily won; he was drowned in this cloud of scent, beauty, and nudity, and she, quite unaware of his thoughts and probably not in the least interested in them, read over the pages quickly and translated full steam ahead:

"He walked over the street and met the gentleman of his friend and said: where do you rush? seeing your face so pale it makes me pain."

The Mémoires had been finished long ago; Alice was now translating another book. Once she came to the lesson an hour earlier, apologising because she had to go to the Little Theatre at seven o'clock. When the lesson was over Vorotov dressed and he too went to the theatre. It seemed to him only for the sake of rest and distraction, and he did not even think of Alice. He would not admit that a serious man, preparing for a scientific career, a stay-at-home, should brush aside his book and rush to the theatre for the sake of meeting an unintellectual, stupid girl whom he hardly knew.

But somehow, dining the intervals his heart beat, and, without noticing it, he ran about the foyer and the corridors like a boy, looking impatiently for someone. Every time the interval was over he was tired, but when he discovered the familiar pink dress and the lovely shoulders veiled with tulle his heart jumped as if from a presentiment of happiness, he smiled joyfully, and for the first time in his life he felt jealous.

Alice was with two ugly students and an officer. She was laughing, talking loudly and evidently flirting. Vorotov had never seen her like that. Apparently she was happy, contented, natural, warm. Why? What was the reason? Perhaps because these people were dear to her and belonged to the same class as she. Vorotov felt the huge abyss between him and that class. He bowed to his teacher, but she nodded coldly and quietly passed by. It was plain she did not want her cavaliers to know that she had pupils and gave lessons because she was poor.

After the meeting at the theatre Vorotov knew that he was in love. During lessons that followed he devoured his elegant teacher with his eyes, and no longer struggling, he gave full rein to his pure and impure thoughts. Alice's face was always cold. Exactly at eight o'clock every evening she said calmly, "Au revoir, Monsieur," and he felt that she was indifferent to him and would remain indifferent, that—his position was hopeless.

Sometimes in the middle of a lesson he would begin dreaming, hoping, building plans; he composed an amorous declaration, remembering that Frenchwomen were frivolous and complaisant, but he had only to give his teacher one glance for his thoughts to be blown out like a candle, when you carry it on to the verandah of a bungalow and the wind is blowing. Once, overcome, forgetting everything, in a frenzy, he could stand it no longer. He barred her way when she came from the study into the hall after the lesson and, losing his breath and stammering, began to declare his love:

"You are dear to me!... I love you. Please let me speak!"

Alice grew pale: probably she was afraid that after this declaration she would not be able to come to him any more and receive a rouble a lesson. She looked at him with terrified eyes and began in a loud whisper:

"Ah, it's impossible! Do not speak, I beg you! Impossible!"

Afterwards Vorotov did not sleep all night; he tortured himself with shame, abused himself, thinking feverishly. He thought that his declaration had offended the girl and that she would not come any more. He made up his mind to find out where she lived from the Address Bureau and to write her an apology. But Alice came without the letter. For a moment she felt awkward, and then opened the book and began to translate quickly, in an animated voice, as always:

"'Oh, young gentleman, do not rend these flowers in my garden which I want to give to my sick daughter.'"

She still goes. Four books have been translated by now but Vorotov knows nothing beyond the word mémoires, and when he is asked about his scientific research work he waves his hand, leaves the question unanswered, and begins to talk about the weather.

A LIVING CALENDAR

State-Councillor Sharamykin's drawing-room is wrapped in a pleasant half-darkness. The big bronze lamp with the green shade, makes the walls, the furniture, the faces, all green, couleur "Nuit d'Ukraine" Occasionally a smouldering log flares up in the dying fire and for a moment casts a red glow over the faces; but this does not spoil the general harmony of light. The general tone, as the painters say, is well sustained.

Sharamykin sits in a chair in front of the fireplace, in the attitude of a man who has just dined. He is an elderly man with a high official's grey side whiskers and meek blue eyes. Tenderness is shed over his face, and his lips are set in a melancholy smile. At his feet, stretched out lazily, with his legs towards the fire-place, Vice-Governor Lopniev sits on a little stool. He is a brave-looking man of about forty. Sharamykin's children are moving about round the piano; Nina, Kolya, Nadya, and Vanya. The door leading to Madame Sharamykin's room is slightly open and the light breaks through timidly. There behind the door sits Sharamykin's wife, Anna Pavlovna, in front of her writing-table. She is president of the local ladies' committee, a lively, piquant lady of thirty years and a little bit over. Through her pince-nez her vivacious black eyes are running over the pages of a French novel. Beneath the novel lies a tattered copy of the report of the committee for last year.

"Formerly our town was much better off in these things," says Sharamykin, screwing up his meek eyes at the glowing coals. "Never a winter passed but some star would pay us a visit. Famous actors and singers used to come ... but now, besides acrobats and organ-grinders, the devil only knows what comes. There's no aesthetic pleasure at all.... We might be living in a forest. Yes.... And does your Excellency remember that Italian tragedian?... What's his name?... He was so dark, and tall.... Let me think.... Oh, yes! Luigi Ernesto di Ruggiero.... Remarkable talent.... And strength. He had only to say one word and the whole theatre was on the qui vive. My darling Anna used to take a great interest in his talent. She hired the theatre for him and sold tickets for the performances in advance.... In return he taught her elocution and gesture. A first-rate fellow! He came here ... to be quite exact ... twelve years ago.... No, that's not true.... Less, ten years.... Anna dear, how old is our Nina?"

"She'll be ten next birthday," calls Anna Pavlovna from her room. "Why?"

"Nothing in particular, my dear. I was just curious.... And good singers used to come. Do you remember Prilipchin, the tenore di grazia? What a charming fellow he was! How good looking! Fair ... a very expressive face, Parisian manners.... And what a voice, your Excellency! Only one weakness: he would sing some notes with his stomach and would take re falsetto—otherwise everything was good. Tamberlik, he said, had taught him.... My dear Anna and I hired a hall for him at the Social Club, and in gratitude for that he used to sing to us for whole days and nights.... He taught dear Anna to sing. He came—I remember it as though it were last night—in Lent, some twelve years ago. No, it's more.... How bad my memory is getting, Heaven help me! Anna dear, how old is our darling Nadya?

"Twelve."

"Twelve ... then we've got to add ten months.... That makes it exact ... thirteen. Somehow there used to be more life in our town then.... Take, for instance, the charity soirées. What enjoyable soirées we used to have before! How elegant! There were singing, playing, and recitation.... After the war, I remember, when the Turkish prisoners were here, dear Anna arranged a soiree on behalf of the wounded. We collected eleven hundred roubles. I remember the Turkish officers were passionately fond of dear Anna's voice, and kissed her hand incessantly. He-he! Asiatics, but a grateful nation. Would you believe me, the soiree was such a success that I wrote an account of it in my diary? It was,—I remember it as though it had only just happened,—in '76,... no, in '77.... No! Pray, when were the Turks here? Anna dear, how old is our little Kolya?"

"I'm seven, Papa!" says Kolya, a brat with a swarthy face and coal black hair.

"Yes, we're old, and we've lost the energy we used to have," Lopniev agreed with a sigh. "That's the real cause. Old age, my friend. No new moving spirits arrive, and the old ones grow old.... The old fire is dull now. When I was younger I did not like company to be bored.... I was your Anna Pavlovna's first assistant. Whether it was a charity soirée or a tombola to support a star who was going to arrive, whatever Anna Pavlovna was arranging, I used to throw over everything and begin to bustle about. One winter, I remember, I bustled and ran so much that I even got ill.... I shan't forget that winter.... Do you remember what a performance we arranged with Anna Pavlovna in aid of the victims of the fire?"

"What year was it?"

"Not so very long ago.... In '79. No, in '80, I believe! Tell me how old is your Vanya?"

"Five," Anna Pavlovna calls from the study.

"Well, that means it was six years ago. Yes, my dear friend, that was a time. It's all over now. The old fire's quite gone."

Lopniev and Sharamykin grew thoughtful. The smouldering log flares up for the last time, and then is covered in ash.

OLD AGE

State-Councillor Usielkov, architect, arrived in his native town, where he had been summoned to restore the cemetery church. He was born in the town, he had grown up and been married there, and yet when he got out of the train he hardly recognised it. Everything was changed. For instance, eighteen years ago, when he left the town to settle in Petersburg, where the railway station is now boys used to hunt for marmots: now as you come into the High Street there is a four storied "Hotel Vienna," with apartments, where there was of old an ugly grey fence. But not the fence or the houses, or anything had changed so much as the people. Questioning the hall-porter, Usielkov discovered that more than half of the people he remembered were dead or paupers or forgotten.

"Do you remember Usielkov?" he asked the porter. "Usielkov, the architect, who divorced his wife.... He had a house in Sviribev Street.... Surely you remember."

"No, I don't remember anyone of the name."

"Why, it's impossible not to remember. It was an exciting case. All the cabmen knew, even. Try to remember. His divorce was managed by the attorney, Shapkin, the swindler ... the notorious sharper, the man who was thrashed at the dub...."

"You mean Ivan Nicolaich?"

"Yes.... Is he alive? dead?"

"Thank heaven, his honour's alive. His honour's a notary now, with an office. Well-to-do. Two houses in Kirpichny Street. Just lately married his daughter off."

Usielkov strode from one corner of the room to another. An idea flashed into his mind. From boredom, he decided to see Shapkin. It was afternoon when he left the hotel and quietly walked to Kirpichny Street. He found Shapkin in his office and hardly recognised him. From the well-built, alert attorney with a quick, impudent, perpetually tipsy expression, Shapkin had become a modest, grey-haired, shrunken old man.

"You don't recognise me.... You have forgotten ...." Usielkov began. "I'm your old client, Usielkov."

"Usielkov? Which Usielkov? Ah!" Remembrance came to Shapkin: he recognised him and was confused. Began exclamations, questions, recollections.

"Never expected ... never thought...." chuckled Shapkin. "What will you have? Would you like champagne? Perhaps you'd like oysters. My dear man, what a lot of money I got out of you in the old days—so much that I can't think what I ought to stand you."

"Please don't trouble," said Usielkov. "I haven't time. I must go to the cemetery and examine the church. I have a commission."

"Splendid. We'll have something to eat and a drink and go together. I've got some splendid horses! I'll take you there and introduce you to the churchwarden.... I'll fix up everything.... But what's the matter, my dearest man? You're not avoiding me, not afraid? Please sit nearer. There's nothing to be afraid of now.... Long ago, I really was pretty sharp, a bit of a rogue ... but now I'm quieter than water, humbler than grass. I've grown old; got a family. There are children.... Time to die!"

The friends had something to eat and drink, and went in a coach and pair to the cemetery.

"Yes, it was a good time," Shapkin was reminiscent, sitting in the sledge. "I remember, but I simply can't believe it. Do you remember how you divorced your wife? It's almost twenty years ago, and you've probably forgotten everything, but I remember it as though I conducted the petition yesterday. My God, how rotten I was! Then I was a smart, casuistical devil, full of sharp practice and devilry.... and I used to run into some shady affairs, particularly when there was a good fee, as in your case, for instance. What was it you paid me then? Five—six hundred. Enough to upset anybody! By the time you left for Petersburg you'd left the whole affair completely in my hands. 'Do what you like!' And your former wife, Sophia Mikhailovna, though she did come from a merchant family, was proud and selfish. To bribe her to take the guilt on herself was difficult—extremely difficult. I used to come to her for a business talk, and when she saw me, she would say to her maid: 'Masha, surely I told you I wasn't at home to scoundrels.' I tried one way, then another ... wrote letters to her, tried to meet her accidentally—no good. I had to work through a third person. For a long time I had trouble with her, and she only yielded when you agreed to give her ten thousand. She could not stand out against ten thousand. She succumbed.... She began to weep, spat in my face, but she yielded and took the guilt on herself."

"If I remember it was fifteen, not ten thousand she took from me," said Usielkov.

"Yes, of course ... fifteen, my mistake." Shapkin was disconcerted. "Anyway it's all past and done with now. Why shouldn't I confess, frankly? Ten I gave to her, and the remaining five I bargained out of you for my own share. I deceived both of you.... It's all past, why be ashamed of it? And who else was there to take from, Boris Pietrovich, if not from you? I ask you.... You were rich and well-to-do. You married in caprice: you were divorced in caprice. You were making a fortune. I remember you got twenty thousand out of a single contract. Whom was I to tap, if not you? And I must confess, I was tortured by envy. If you got hold of a nice lot of money, people would take off their hats to you: but the same people would beat me for shillings and smack my face in the club. But why recall it? It's time to forget."

"Tell me, please, how did Sophia Mikhailovna live afterwards?"

"With her ten thousand? On ne peut plus badly.... God knows whether it was frenzy or pride and conscience that tortured her, because she had sold herself for money—or perhaps she loved you; but, she took to drink, you know. She received the money and began to gad about with officers in troikas.... Drunkenness, philandering, debauchery.... She would come into a tavern with an officer, and instead of port or a light wine, she would drink the strongest cognac to drive her into a frenzy."

"Yes, she was eccentric. I suffered enough with her. She would take offence at some trifle and then get nervous.... And what happened afterwards?"

"A week passed, a fortnight.... I was sitting at home writing. Suddenly, the door opened and she comes in. 'Take your cursed money,' she said, and threw the parcel in my face.... She could not resist it.... Five hundred were missing. She had only got rid of five hundred."

"And what did you do with the money?"

"It's all past and done with. What's the good of concealing it?... I certainly took it. What are you staring at me like that for? Wait for the sequel. It's a complete novel, the sickness of a soul! Two months passed by. One night I came home drunk, in a wicked mood.... I turned on the light and saw Sophia Mikhailovna sitting on my sofa, drunk too, wandering a bit, with something savage in her face as if she had just escaped from the mad-house. 'Give me my money back,' she said. 'I've changed my mind. If I'm going to the dogs, I want to go madly, passionately. Make haste, you scoundrel, give me the money.' How indecent it was!"

"And you ... did you give it her?"

"I remember I gave her ten roubles."

"Oh ... is it possible?" Usielkov frowned. "If you couldn't do it yourself, or you didn't want to, you could have written to me.... And I didn't know ... I didn't know."

"My dear man, why should I write, when she wrote herself afterwards when she was in hospital?"

"I was so taken up with the new marriage that I paid no attention to letters.... But you were an outsider; you had no antagonism to Sophia Mikhailovna.... Why didn't you help her?"

"We can't judge by our present standards, Boris Pietrovich. Now we think in this way; but then we thought quite differently.... Now I might perhaps give her a thousand roubles; but then even ten roubles ... she didn't get them for nothing. It's a terrible story. It's time to forget.... But here you are!"

The sledge stopped at the churchyard gate. Usielkov and Shapkin got out of the sledge, went through the gate and walked along a long, broad avenue. The bare cherry trees, the acacias, the grey crosses and monuments sparkled with hoar-frost. In each flake of snow the bright sunny day was reflected. There was the smell you find in all cemeteries of incense and fresh-dug earth.

"You have a beautiful cemetery," said Usielkov. "It's almost an orchard."

"Yes, but it's a pity the thieves steal the monuments. Look, there, behind that cast-iron memorial, on the right, Sophia Mikhailovna is buried. Would you like to see?"

The friends turned to the right, stepping in deep snow towards the cast-iron memorial.

"Down here," said Shapkin, pointing to a little stone of white marble. "Some subaltern or other put up the monument on her grave." Usielkov slowly took off his hat and showed his bald pate to the snow. Eying him, Shapkin also took off his hat, and another baldness shone beneath the sun. The silence round about was like the tomb, as though the air were dead, too. The friends looked at the stone, silent, thinking.

"She is asleep!" Shapkin broke the silence. "And she cares very little that she took the guilt upon herself and drank cognac. Confess, Boris Pietrovich!"

"What?" asked Usielkov, sternly.

"That, however loathsome the past may be, it's better than this." And Shapkin pointed to his grey hairs.

"In the old days I did not even think of death.... If I'd met her, I would have circumvented her, but now ... well, now!"

Sadness took hold of Usielkov. Suddenly he wanted to cry, passionately, as he once desired to love.... And he felt that these tears would be exquisite, refreshing. Moisture came out of his eyes and a lump rose in his throat, but.... Shapkin was standing by his side, and Usielkov felt ashamed of his weakness before a witness. He turned back quickly and walked towards the church.

Two hours later, having arranged with the churchwarden and examined the church, he seized the opportunity while Shapkin was talking away to the priest, and ran to shed a tear. He walked to the stone surreptitiously, with stealthy steps, looking round all the time. The little white monument stared at him absently, so sadly and innocently, as though a girl and not a wanton divorcée were beneath.

"If I could weep, could weep!" thought Usielkov.

But the moment for weeping had been lost. Though the old man managed to make his eyes shine, and tried to bring himself to the right pitch, the tears did not flow and the lump did not rise in his throat.... After waiting for about ten minutes, Usielkov waved his arm and went to look for Shapkin.

www.ingramcontent.com/pod-product-compliance
Ingram Content Group UK Ltd.
Pitfield, Milton Keynes, MK11 3LW, UK
UKHW041823200726
13854UKWH00002BA/530

9 789388 841566